IN THE SWIM

MOLLIE THOMPSON

Pathfinders

Scripture Union

Other books by this author

Rat Pack – *Impressions* series
A Letter for Emma – *Leopard* series
The Lost Donkey – *6–8s*

© Mollie Thompson
First published 1996

Published by Scripture Union, 207–209 Queensway,
Bletchley, Milton Keynes, MK2 2EB, England.

ISBN 0 86201 920 6

British Library Cataloguing-in-Publication Data.
A catalogue record for this book is available from the British Library.

Phototypeset by Intype London Ltd
Printed and bound in Great Britian by Cox & Wyman Ltd, Reading.

~ 1 ~

They were the first things that Pip noticed as the car turned in at the front gate: milk bottles – two of them – still on the doorstep.

The family had set off very early that morning and it had been a long day; such a sad day too. Pip had never been to a funeral before; she'd only been a little girl when Grandma died, and now Grandpa had gone.

She looked again at the milk bottles standing there like soldiers, the evening sunlight sending their tall, straight shadows up against the door. Grandpa had been in the army and he'd always walked with a straight back, not stooped like some old people. Even the last few photographs had shown him tall and erect, looking healthy and smiling into the camera.

'You forgot to take the milk in. It'll be sour by now.'

Her mother turned to look at her. 'Oh Philippa, don't you think I've had more on my mind today than milk bottles?' she said wearily.

'Sorry Mum. I should have said *we* forgot.'

She jumped out of the car and removed the bottles while Dad opened the front door. The house was very quiet and still but that seemed right somehow; it fitted their mood. They had driven most of the way back in silence and, now that they were home again, there still didn't seem to be anything that any of them wanted to say.

At last Dad broke the silence. 'How about a nice pot of tea? I'll put the kettle on.'

Pip could hear him clattering cups and saucers around in the kitchen and wondered if she should go and help, but she didn't. She stayed with her mum instead, sitting on the arm of the chair and feeling very awkward. She wanted to say something comforting but she didn't want to set her off crying again. Besides, she felt a lot like crying herself.

She realised that sometimes things don't need to be spoken as Mum reached out and patted her daughter's arm and they smiled at each other. Then Pip let her thoughts drift away again.

She realised too just how much she loved Grandpa Rhodes, for lots of reasons, but mainly because he'd always treated her like a person and not like a child. Even when she was little he'd made a point of answering her questions as if they were very important; as if what a small girl had thought about really mattered to him. She was going to miss him very much.

The tea revived the Johnson family and gradually they each relaxed in their own way. Dad went to inspect the tomatoes in the greenhouse and Mum began to prepare the evening meal. Perhaps having something to do helped them to take their minds off things.

Pip sighed.

Mum had said, 'No thank you dear, I can manage,' to Pip's offer of help.

Since she hadn't anything that she *must* do, she went up to her bedroom, looking for something that she might do. Taking the day off school to attend her grandpa's funeral meant that she hadn't any fresh work assignments – but there was still her history coursework to complete.

Should she phone Natalie about borrowing that book? No, tomorrow would do.

Pip glanced across at her cassettes stacked in their carousel. She could tidy them into 'best loved' order or into alphabetical order. She could listen to the one she'd bought last week.

With her hand poised to pick up the cassette, she suddenly realised that her taste in music must reveal a lot about the kind of person she was. What did this one say about her? she wondered. 'Oooz Dance Mix' by Malcolm and the Mud Wrestlers. She grinned to herself. Grandpa would have had something comical to say about that title, she felt sure.

He had liked military music – brass bands with a lot of 'oompa', as he called it – and he also liked church music with those rich harmonies that always go just where you expect them to go.

With a sudden catch in her breath, Pip remembered that all the music that they'd heard that afternoon at the service had been chosen by Grandpa, well in advance. But that was so like him, to plan his own funeral down to the last detail, as if he'd been responsible for a military campaign.

She felt the tears well up in her eyes and spill over. 'Why do nice people have to die?' she muttered under her breath – replaying the question she'd once asked him long ago. She would always remember his matter-of-fact reply.

'Because after a few hundred years the world would get rather full, wouldn't it? Besides,' he had confided, '. . . I'm quite looking forward to discovering some of the things that Jesus promised us.'

Dear Grandpa, he always saw everything as a new adventure, something to explore.

Pip found she could smile through her tears. Grandpa always met things head-on and faced what was coming. Now it was her turn to face the fact that he had gone.

She slipped out of the dark-grey skirt and peeled off the black jumper which covered her plain white blouse. Rummaging through her wardrobe she chose a pale-blue overshirt and her orange floral leggings, then she looked at herself in the long mirror.

She was tall, thin and angular. Her fair hair, hanging down almost to her waist in one thick plait, seemed to make her look even taller. She stared back at her reflection and nodded to it, feeling that the change out of those dark, sombre clothes was making her feel brighter inside too.

Out of her bedroom window she could see next door's cat lying curled up and nearly hidden by the purple fronds of a catmint plant. He was enjoying the last warmth of the evening sun before it disappeared behind the garden shed. Grandpa had had a cat too, called Major Tom. She remembered how the elderly puss used to lie in wait on the wall and 'bop' people on the head as they went past. Grandpa had always claimed that Major Tom had a sharper sense of humour than some humans.

As she stood there in her bedroom, it seemed that everything she thought about led her mind straight back to Grandpa. Even the row of silver and bronze badges and trophies on the long wooden shelf were only there because of him. Of course, it was Pip who had won them by her own efforts, but it had been Grandpa who had taught her to swim in the first place.

He had spent hours with her when she was really small, swimming up and down the shallow part of Ballantyne Lake, while Grandma sat patiently knitting underneath a large green sunshade. Then the warm friction of the rough towel and the even warmer comfort of hot soup from a Thermos jug. She had enjoyed her swimming then.

'Philippa, come down now, supper is nearly ready,' her dad's voice called.

Pip closed her bedroom door carefully and came down the stairs, two shallow steps at a time. She moved through into the dining-room and began to set the table: three square raffia mats and place settings, three oval raffia mats and serving spoons, three brown tumblers and tiny round mats beneath them.

When she went into the kitchen to fill the water jug, Dad was rinsing his soil-coated hands under the tap and Mum was filling the serving dishes. She looked tired and the dark wisps of hair that had escaped from tidiness were moist with the steam from the vegetables. Although she was still wearing the full-skirted black dress that she'd worn at the funeral, it was now covered by a butcher's striped apron.

'Oh, you've changed your clothes,' she said, and Pip thought she caught the faintest hint of disapproval in her mother's voice. Perhaps she only imagined that. She looked down at her flowered leggings and shrugged her shoulders.

'Well, I felt all depressed in dark colours.'

Her mother just looked at her and sighed, then busied herself with the vegetables again. It made Pip wonder if perhaps she'd been a bit insensitive after all.

Dad followed her back into the dining-room, smiled at her and straightened one of the table mats as Pip's water jug nudged it out of place.

'Your grandpa always liked bright colours,' he said quietly.

'Yes he did, didn't he?' Pip replied, grateful for this small comment. It helped to put things back into perspective somehow.

After the meal was eaten and cleared away, the rather strained atmosphere gradually began to clear. It was only natural that Mum should be feeling sad and quiet. After all, Grandpa was her father and so it must be even worse for her.

Pip looked across at her own father sitting there; he was strong and quiet but always there for them when they needed him. In contrast to his quietness, Mum was usually vivacious and full of ideas and opinions. But not today. Now she sat in the chair over by the French windows, staring out across the lawn and down to where the fish-pond lay, in a small hollow surrounded by reeds and water iris.

'Are you all right, Mum? Is there anything I can get you?'

She looked up and the faintest touch of a smile crossed her face.

'I'm fine, love, really I am. I was just remembering the day your grandpa helped Dad to dig out the pond.'

Pip flopped down on the couch, then leant forward, elbows on knees.

'I can just remember that. Didn't he fall in while you were filling it with water?'

'He did indeed,' Dad joined in, 'and Grandma had to drive him home wrapped in an old bath towel.'

They all looked at each other and laughed.

'It's good to remember happy times,' Pip said thoughtfully. 'And there are so many stored in my head – it's almost like a set of photos.'

Dad brushed back a lock of hair which had fallen across his forehead and stood for a moment, hand on head. It was a little habit he'd grown into and it made him look like one of those cartoon characters with a thought balloon saying 'Thinks!!'.

Mum looked questioningly at him.

'Didn't we have some slides somewhere, Angela?'

'I think they're up in the spare room on that shelf,' she replied.

Dad was through the doorway and halfway up the stairs when she called after him, 'Bring the photo albums too. Did you hear me, Matthew?'

'I heard you!' he called back.

They spent the rest of the evening going through recorded memories dating back many years. They could see Grandma and Grandpa standing with proud smiles and the winning dahlias at their local flower show. Some of the photos were in an assorted jumble spanning the years, while others had been neatly catalogued behind the transparent sheets of photo albums.

'Look at *these*,' Pip said, all excitement. 'It's Grandpa's visit to the Holy Land. Doesn't he look young?'

Mum came and looked over her shoulder. 'Well yes, these were taken over forty years ago.'

As Pip turned the pages of the big leather-bound photo album she could remember Grandpa telling her about Jerusalem and Nazareth and the shores of Lake Galilee. She could almost hear his voice as he had described the sights and sounds to her. She had been very small at the time but the memory was still sharp and clear. He had described to her how he had felt as he walked on the same stony ground that Jesus may once have trodden; how the smells of cooking fires and freshly caught fish down by that vast inland lake would have been exactly the same 2,000 years ago. Grandpa had made the New Testament stories come alive for her when he told them. She imagined she could feel the heat of the desert and the refreshing coolness of the River Jordan; she could even imagine what it must have felt like to be one of the people in the crowd on the mountainside, listening to Jesus speaking to them.

'Come back, Pip, you're miles away,' Dad said, touching her gently on the shoulder.

She turned to him. 'Yes, I was. I was remembering the way Grandpa used to describe things when we looked at these photos together.'

Mum smiled to herself. She too had memories of her father's tales of travels and adventures when he was younger – tales of Egypt and of India.

'He once told me about a time when he was in India. He and his friends were swimming in some river and a herd of elephants came down to the water's edge to drink. The swimmers scrambled out on the far bank rather rapidly, and wouldn't you!'

That reference to swimming brought Mum back to the present.

'You aren't taking the car tomorrow, are you?' she

asked her husband. 'Because Philippa and I need to be at the Lido by eight o'clock.'

He reassured her that he'd go by train.

Neither of them saw the expression on Pip's face because she was careful to hide it from them. Swimming practice *again*. Two-and-a-half hours of slogging up and down the pool, pushing herself until her muscles ached, trying to knock another quarter of a second off her lap time. She groaned inwardly at the prospect, but kept her thoughts to herself.

'I think I'll go up to bed now. It's been a long day,' she said.

Mum kissed her goodnight and said, 'God Bless,' just as she always did.

Dad gave her long plait a playful tug and said, 'Hang on kid.' This was an old joke between them.

It almost seemed like any other night – except that it wasn't. And yet Pip knew that this was what Grandpa would have wanted.

'Take each day as it comes,' he would have said. 'And put your best foot forward.'

She smiled as she flicked off her bedside light. So which is a swimmer's best foot? Probably my backstroke – she thought.

~ 2 ~

There was hardly anyone about at the Lido, only a couple of serious swimmers like herself. The sploshers and splashers didn't usually arrive before ten o'clock which was why Mum always made sure they got an early start on a Saturday morning. After depositing Pip outside the main entrance, Mum would depart – leaving the car somewhere central – and spend the morning drinking coffee with friends or doing a bit of shopping.

Pip stood in the empty changing-rooms, putting her hair into two plaits and winding them around her head until they made a thick coronet. She'd done it so often that her fingers twisted and turned without her even thinking about it. An elastic band completed the operation, then she glanced at herself in the wall-mirror as she passed.

Grandpa had always called her 'my little Esther Williams' with her hair done like this. He had once shown her a faded newspaper article showing the smiling swimmer with her hair wrapped around her head in that distinctive style, and Pip had copied it ever since. Better than trying to push my hair into one of those rubber skull caps, she thought as she stepped through the foot-bath and out into the pool area.

She could see Andy at the far end of the pool, rising and lunging in an effortless butterfly stroke that ate up the distance between them. As his head bobbed up at the end of his lane she waved to him.

'Where were you the other day?' he asked, prising himself half-out of the water on his elbows.

'A family crisis – I couldn't get here,' she replied.

It wasn't that she didn't want to tell him but she didn't feel like going into all the details just at present.

He nodded and submerged, leaving Pip standing on the edge. She looked along the pool, noticing that there was only the elderly Mr Potts – with the white hair and the sunburnt pate – solemnly ploughing along between the anchored lines of blue and white floats. Idly she wondered if she'd still be doing the same at his age – she doubted it.

Once in the water, it was almost as though she switched on to autopilot, the limbs coordinated and the energy released in measured doses. There was no thought required, only the slow intake and expulsion of air powered by lungs that had grown accustomed to what was expected of them. Back and forth, lap after lap, Pip moved with the ease and grace of a dolphin – but hardly with a dolphin's speed. No, it was her speed that she was supposed to be working on.

At that moment she became aware that her coach, Jim Parrish, was leaning against the diving-board watching her, his lips drawn into a tight line.

'And is that your best effort then?'

'I was only warming up,' she said in defence.

'Oh, and shall I boil a kettle for you?' he said with a sarcastic smile. He was trying to needle her into action and Pip resented it.

She said nothing as she took up her starting position, waiting tense and alert for the sharp trill of his whistle. Then she drove forward with all the pent-up energy of a coiled spring.

The crawl was not the stroke she excelled at but this time she was determined to give a good account of herself. She slowed on the turn, which lost her valuable seconds, but even so her time was quite adequate to make it into the relay team.

'Better,' was his grudging praise. 'Now let me see your backstroke – and put some beef into it.'

After twenty minutes of work against the stopwatch, Pip's concentration began to wander. She knew she was good, in fact on backstroke she was the fastest in the team, and yet Jim Parrish wouldn't let up on her. He kept the pressure on, always finding new ways to goad her into action. It wasn't just with her; he did the same thing to everyone, but that wasn't the point. She'd worked her socks off for the encouragement and praise, but now . . . sarcasm!

Something inside Pip just shrivelled. Why was she here? Why should she put in all these hours just to be moaned at by a has-been whose speed could be matched by a turtle with three legs? The answer snapped into her mind almost immediately – she was here because Mum and Dad paid for her to be trained by one of the best coaches in the county; no longer light in years but heavy in experience. Even so – that didn't give him the right to mock her.

Pip hauled herself out of the pool, water streaming off her sleek-suited body and sun-bronzed legs. She reached for the towel hanging limply over the barrier separating spectators from swimmers, then moved towards the exit.

'Hey, where are you off to in such a hurry?' Jim demanded.

She looked up at the clock, drawing his attention to the time.

'I only work union hours!' she said, deciding to fight fire with fire.

The last view she had of him was one of open-mouthed surprise as she pushed open the swing doors and left. Well, serve him right! she thought.

The remainder of Saturday was unremarkable. A phone call to Natalie provided the information that the promised book was still at school, but that they'd been allowed a further two weeks before the history coursework was due in.

Sunday filled itself with this and that: she sat out in the garden on the swing hammock and read for a while, then, feeling that Mum might appreciate some cheerful company, she went into the kitchen and made a gooseberry crumble and two loaves of banana bread – Natalie's recipe.

Monday morning was damp and dismal. When Pip got into school, several of her group made a mumbled reference to Friday and asked if everything went all right. They meant well but were embarrassed to ask about the funeral.

'Yes, thank you,' she said, and the matter was closed.

Natalie on the other hand had said all that needed to be said on the subject when they were on the phone. Today something more immediate was on her mind.

'One thing I forgot to tell you,' Natalie continued as if the conversation hadn't had a thirty-six hour interval, 'was that on Friday, Mr Brennan made an announcement in the hall.'

Pip waited for the revelation.

'He is going to organise a computer club and he's put a sheet on the notice-board for anyone who's interested.'

'And you've enrolled, right?' Pip felt this was a fairly safe guess knowing Natalie's passion for computers.

They walked down the corridor together and found quite a number of their year clustered around the notice-board.

'Not only that. I've put your name down too, see – next to mine. I did it because it's probably a first-come-first-served thing, and you not being here on Friday I thought . . .' Her voice trailed away as she watched her friend's face for a response.

Pip was reading the notice again, more carefully this time.

'I'd have loved to but . . . it's on a Wednesday, and that's my swimming night.'

'Oh Pip, what a pain! Is there no chance then?'

'I'll have a word with Mum but it's not very hopeful. The team trials are only three weeks away, and there's already been a bit of unpleasantness from Jim – you know, my coach.'

As they stood talking quietly about their disappointment, they were overheard by a group of boys from Year Eleven. One boy gave a sneering laugh.

'What's your problem? Won't *coachy* let you off the lead then?'

One of his mates chimed in with, 'Well, if it isn't Pip-the-Porpoise – they train you to jump through hoops don't they?'

And another voice added, 'I thought it was balancing balls on noses.'

Pip could feel her anger rising but she had sense enough to know that there was no point in rising to their stupid taunts.

'Come on Natalie, let's go. I'll talk to you later,' she said, taking her friend's arm and leaving the jeering lads behind.

'*Idiots!*' said Natalie vehemently. 'Take no notice of them.'

'I'm not,' Pip said. Even so, there was a part of her still smarting from the insults. After all, there might be just a grain of truth in it. In a sense she did jump through hoops and balance balls on her nose – because it seemed to make Mum and Dad happy. But was that a good enough reason any more? It used to make her happy too but now . . .

'Not any more!' Her voice was surprisingly defiant, even to her own ears.

'Pardon?' Natalie said.

'Nothing, I was just thinking aloud.'

There were times during the day when Pip felt sure Natalie was about to mention Computer Club again, but she never actually let the words out of her mouth. Pip was grateful because it was a sore point and, as the day wore on, she made up her mind to tackle her parents that very evening.

All the way home on the bus she silently practised

imaginary conversations in her head, going through what she would say and what they might reply, until she'd finally worked out an opening gambit.

When she got home, Mum was working in the back garden, which was good because Pip had already decided that it would be better to approach the subject very casually at first.

'I'm back, Mum!' she called from the back door.

Her mother looked up and waved a gloved hand. 'I'm just dead-heading these few roses,' she said as Pip walked down the path.

'Mum, I've got piles of work to do on my Elizabethan Theatre project. Do you think Dad would let me use his PC some time?'

'His what, dear?'

'His computer. It's so much faster than writing it all out by hand.'

'Oh, you mustn't go in there without your dad being here,' Mum said.

It was an unwritten rule that nobody touched anything in the little back bedroom because, now that he was working from home, Mr Johnson used it as an office. Even Mum wouldn't vac or dust in there in case she disturbed important papers, but occasionally she would prop the vac up against the door – as a gentle hint – which Dad usually took.

'Of course I won't go in. I was just wondering, that's all.'

Pip grinned to herself as she went back inside; at least she'd managed to introduce the subject of computers and that would make the follow-up a little easier, she thought.

The follow-up when it came was not at all what Pip was expecting. Apparently Mum had been listening quite carefully to Pip and had mentioned it to Dad as soon as he returned home. The first thing that Pip knew was a tap on her bedroom door.

'Are you busy?' he asked, popping his head around the half-open door. 'Oh, I can see you are.'

There were books piled high on the bedside table, papers lying higgledy-piggledy all across the duvet, with Pip sitting cross-legged in the middle of them, and an assortment of pens, pencils and crayons up-ended in a favourite old mug which had lost its handle. Dad smiled as he picked his way carefully across the rug which looked as if it was being used as a floor-level desk.

'Your mother's been telling me that you want to use my computer and printer for a school project you're doing. Well, that's not very practical because I need it myself most of the time. However, perhaps we could get you a small PC of your own. How about that?'

Before Pip had time to react or respond in any way Dad slipped in his little proviso.

'But before we say any more, I want you to promise me faithfully that you won't let it interfere with your swimming. A computer can, all too easily, become a champion time-waster if you're not very careful.'

In the space of a few seconds Dad had picked up her idea, processed it and returned it to her in a form which she wasn't prepared for. Asking to borrow his PC had been more in the way of a lead-in to the subject than a real need. What she really wanted was to join the computer club with Natalie and to spend some time doing something that *wasn't* swimming. Now Dad was asking her to make him a promise that she didn't want to keep. What's the use of a gift if it has strings attached? she thought crossly.

'Is it a promise?' her dad asked quietly.

Pip didn't know how to get out of this situation. Yes, she'd like her own computer but more than that she wanted her freedom. She was already feeling the pace at school hotting up as exams loomed nearer, and every other bit of spare time was taken up with swimming. When could she be herself and do what *she* wanted to do for a change? She bit furiously at the end of her pencil and shook her head. Dad frowned at her.

'Does that mean no? Well I'm sorry, no promise – no computer. We can't let your swimming suffer.'

'Dad, that's not it!' she said helplessly.

'What is it then? Don't you want a computer?'

'I hadn't even thought of one of my own – I just wanted to join Computer Club at school, that's all.'

While they'd been talking Mum had come upstairs, probably expecting to find Pip's face wreathed in smiles at Dad's offer. Instead she found her daughter looking glum and her husband looking bewildered.

'And is that a problem?' Dad continued.

Pip looked up, saw her mum standing in the doorway and shrugged her shoulders. 'It's Wednesday after school,' she said and waited for what she knew would follow.

'What about Wednesday? That's swimming practice night,' Mum said sharply.

'Couldn't I swim another evening?'

'No, of course not, don't be silly. It's all been arranged to fit in with the other fixtures. You know that.'

'Computer Club is only every other week.'

Pip looked at her dad, hoping that perhaps he might

help her. But no, he stood firmly on Mum's side of the rapidly developing argument.

'It's a matter of priorities,' he said pompously. 'You've only got a limited amount of time available; there are your forthcoming exams and then any other free time you have must be for your swimming.'

Pip could contain her rising anger no longer. At the mention of the words 'free time' she gave an explosive snort of derision.

'*Free*? What's free about it? Go here, do this, do that! Jump in, jump out! And Jim Parrish is beginning to get up my nose too – always pushing. Now *this*! Computer Club is only two hours for goodness' sake. Can't I even be allowed *two* hours of what *I* want for a change?'

'Take that look off your face, Philippa!' Mum said sternly.

'Oh *great*, I can't even do what I want with my own face now,' she snapped back.

Dad moved towards the door. 'If you're going to be rude there's no point in talking to you,' he said sadly as he and Mum left the room.

As soon as their footsteps faded away along the landing, Pip realised what she'd done and it made her feel awful. Dad had come upstairs quite prepared to buy her her own computer and she'd ungraciously flung his kindness back in his face. And Mum had only asked Dad about borrowing his computer because she'd thought it would help Pip with her work.

'I've done it *again*,' she muttered and kicked the bedside table as she passed. The carelessly piled books slowly collapsed in a heap on the floor.

As she bent to pick them up, she thought back over the last few hours and wondered why it was that things seemed to be collapsing in her life too. She loved her mum and her dad and she knew they loved her, and yet so often these days there were rows and unpleasant-nesses which blew up over nothing. But was it over nothing?

Surely she had a right to make some decisions of her own? And staying on two hours after school for Computer Club hardly seemed like the crime of the century. But looking at it another way – both Mum and Dad had given up things that they wanted in order to pay for her swimming tours and special tuition. They wanted her to be successful.

'I just wish it mattered to me as much as it does to them.'

Pip sighed and tidied up the papers scattered across her bed. She knew she couldn't stay up in her room sulking and the sooner she went downstairs to apologise, the better it would be for everyone.

All it took was the simple statement 'I'm sorry' and as soon as she'd said it – and really meant it – she could feel a warmth returning to the room. They were a family who were always ready to forgive and forget.

'I didn't mean to be so ungrateful,' she said quietly.

Both Mum and Dad told her that it was all right, that maybe they were all tired, that she'd probably been working too hard upstairs and asked if she would like a mug of coffee.

Yes, she would – a cup of coffee was a panacea for all ills!

~ 3 ~

Natalie stared at her friend in disbelief.

'And you turned it down? Your dad offers to buy you your own computer and you say no? That has to be the most stupid thing I ever heard!'

Pip shrugged her shoulders and drew her lips into a pout. She watched as Natalie threw herself into one of her theatrical routines, tossing her black curls and flinging her arms wide in a display of assumed emotion.

'What I wouldn't give for my own computer,' she moaned. 'Every byte, every bus would be mine and mine alone – to do with as I pleased.'

Pip let her chatter on for a while and then she gasped, 'Natalie, shut up, it wasn't like that – it had strings attached and I couldn't accept it.'

'So? Tied up in strings or ribbons and bows – what difference does it make?'

'Be serious for a minute and I'll tell you.'

After Pip had finished telling her the full story,

Natalie sat down on the grassy bank at the far end of the playing field and motioned Pip to sit next to her. She had a purposeful and yet remote expression on her face, as if thinking was taking all her available energy.

'What we need is a plan of action,' she said at last.

Pip raised her eyebrows questioningly.

'If reasoning won't influence them we shall just have to be underhand about it,' Natalie said grinning. 'You know – evade the issue.'

'I don't think it'll work with Mum.'

'You haven't heard the plan yet.'

Natalie's roguish smile made Pip laugh and even though she was somewhat hesitant about trying to trick her mum, she found herself listening for what her friend would say next.

'What you need is an ally – and that's me. Surely between us we can manage to get you into Computer Club without too much trouble.'

'Yes but—' Pip began.

'No buts. Come on, be a rebel. It's not as though we'll be doing anything really wrong.'

Pip was still uneasy but deep down it was quite exciting to be striking a blow for freedom, and there was something about Natalie's enthusiasm that had fuelled her own imagination. Pip listened to Natalie's idea with growing amazement, but would she really dare to fly in the face of authority like that? Well, she could give it a try.

Only two days to wait.

As soon as she walked into the school building on Wednesday morning, Pip saw Natalie standing by the swing doors. She winked and Natalie raised one thumb in reply; this was their 'plot' signal, telling Pip that Natalie's mother would be picking them both up from the bottom of the school drive. Pip knew that the rest of it was up to her and she wondered if she'd be able to play the part convincingly. An army of butterflies fluttered around in her stomach at the thought of what lay ahead but she couldn't back out now.

Halfway through the morning, Pip excused herself from the room, walked along the top corridor and down the stairs until she reached the fourth step from the bottom. With great care she staged a fall, spreading herself out with her right leg stretched out and her left leg tucked underneath herself. The steps were cold, hard and very uncomfortable but with a bit of luck she wouldn't be there for too long. It wouldn't matter who found her as long as they raised the alarm, but seconds stretched into minutes and still nobody came.

After a while Pip began to feel the pins and needles starting in the twisted leg and she thought, with a wry smile, that if she tried to walk now she really would fall down. This was ridiculous; was the school staircase always as deserted as this at eleven o'clock in the morning?

She left it for a little while longer before deciding that she'd have to take more positive action. Her left leg had really gone to sleep now but she managed to ease the shoe off a very uncomfortable foot and, with a mighty effort, she hurled it over the banisters, straight at the headmaster's door. It hit the door with a thud.

Pip lay there waiting. Someone was sure to hear

that, and even if Mr Morris wasn't in, his secretary was sure to be. The door opened and little Mrs Ealing came out, took one look at the shoe then noticed Pip's arm hanging loosely between the banister rails.

Everything happened very speedily after that. She was retrieved from her prone position and half-carried to the rest-room, checked thoroughly for bone breakage, anointed with witch-hazel to prevent bruising and provided with a cup of sweet tea to combat shock. She obligingly tried to walk but grimaced with pain and mumbled words to the effect that she'd 'pulled a muscle'. Everyone was very sympathetic, she was entered in the Accident Book with due solemnity and they let her lie down on the bed in the rest-room because she said she felt faint.

As soon as the lunch bell went, Natalie's face appeared round the door.

'Poor old you!' she said laughing. 'What a *surprising* thing to happen.'

Fortunately this strange comment was not noticed by Mrs Ealing who'd come in behind Natalie to check on the patient.

'Do you feel like eating any lunch?' Mrs Ealing asked.

'I could manage a little I think,' Pip replied, silently aware of the pangs of hunger that always hit her at about this time.

'I'll help you to the dining-room,' Natalie quickly volunteered. 'You can lean on me and hop on your good leg.'

Pip acted the part like a professional, limping and looking pained whenever there was someone there to witness the performance. She did it so well that not one of her form-mates realised what a fraud she was.

In fact, over the lunch table, one or two of them asked if she wouldn't be better going home.

As the whole point of the exercise was to stay at school even longer today, all she said to them was, 'I'll be all right,' and adopted a martyred expression.

When they were alone, Natalie thrust a tiny tartan make-up bag into Pip's hand.

'You look far too healthy. Here, rub some blusher on your eyelids, it'll make them look puffy. And isn't it about time you phoned your mum?'

Pip rolled her eyes and sighed. 'This is going to be the difficult bit – but here goes. Wait for me outside Room 61.' She hobbled away leaving Natalie grinning widely.

When she knocked on his door, it was Mr Morris's gruff voice that said, 'Come in.' He willingly agreed that she could use the phone in the outer office. Mrs Ealing nodded and smiled, then obligingly ceased the rapid chatter of her typewriter.

Although Pip and Natalie had rehearsed what she was going to say, the moment she heard her mother's voice on the other end of the phone, a sort of paralysis seized her throat muscles. At last she managed to gasp out, 'It's me Mum. I've fallen down the school stairs. I'm phoning from Mr Morris's office.'

After that, the conversation went almost as they'd anticipated for a while: sympathy . . . How had it happened? . . . Had she been running? How badly was she hurt? Once again, Pip used the magic words 'pulled muscle' but this time their magic failed.

'Oh that's not too bad, at least there are no bones broken,' Mum said cheerfully. 'You don't want me to come for you now, do you? You can last out for the rest of the afternoon, can't you?'

Pip took a deep breath and launched into phase two of the plan. She explained that she didn't think she'd be fit for swimming practice, but that if she stayed a little while after school Natalie's mother would meet them and bring her home afterwards.

There was silence for a few moments – which to Pip seemed like an eternity – then Mum answered.

'Nonsense dear – the water will ease any pain and stop you stiffening up. We can get Jim to take a look at it too, he knows more about muscles than most folk do. Besides, we couldn't possibly put Mrs Orwell to all that trouble.'

Pip's hasty, 'But Mum . . .' had no effect since her mum was already saying that she'd be collected at the usual time.

The receiver was replaced with a click of finality and there was nothing more that Pip could do. She couldn't even relieve her feeling with a quick curse or stamp of the foot – not with Mrs Ealing hovering around.

She was so fed-up that she almost forgot to limp along to Room 61 where Natalie was waiting. One look at Pip's face told Natalie that things had not gone well.

'Well, that's that for this week. Never mind, we'll just have to come up with something else,' Natalie said.

Pip pulled a face, then they went into the classroom together.

'You're forgetting to hobble,' Natalie whispered out of the corner of her mouth.

'What's the point now?'

'You've got to keep in character; any good actor will tell you that.'

At a quarter to four, Mum's car was parked across the road from the school entrance. Remembering Natalie's advice, Pip limped across the road and opened the car door. Mum gave her usual greeting, then she asked if her leg felt any better.

She seemed sympathetic and yet there was just a hint of impatience behind her voice. Pip wondered if she should drop the charade after all. Despite what Natalie had said, maybe there was no point in pretending any longer.

'It's a lot better thanks,' she told her mother.

'Pip, what has happened between you and Jim? After hearing him on the phone, I'm wondering if he'll even be bothered to check you over.'

Pip could feel her cheeks beginning to redden. Obviously when Mum phoned he must have told her about the outburst last week; she hadn't exactly been rude, but what Dad would have called 'impudent'.

'I got in a bit of a state last week,' she admitted.

'So I believe,' was all her mother said.

The rest of the girls' team arrived in ones and twos and the chatter in the changing-rooms revolved around the impending trip which had been arranged to coincide with half-term holiday. Pip listened and added the occasional remark when it seemed necessary but her mind was on other things. As it happened, there wasn't anything else in particular that she'd wanted to do this half-term, but it would have been all the same if there had been. It was just assumed that all the swimming team would go on this trip around the countryside, visiting the facilities used by the other competing teams. Nobody had asked if she wanted to go; they'd just assumed that she'd be going because she'd always done what was expected of her.

She stood at the edge of the pool, taking no part in the chatter and laughter going on around her. She looked up and over the pool, her eyes following the pale-blue painted metal roof supports until she could see the café, high above the water and safe behind its glass windows. Mum was there, meeting with the other parents, discussing last minute details for the trip and drinking coffee. Angie's mother was holding forth about something and waving a sheet of paper in the air – probably the list of hotels and guest-houses where rooms had been booked. Apparently it would be the luck of the draw who got to go where.

Pip sighed loudly.

'What's the matter with you? You look fed up,' said a voice. She turned and saw that Andy had come up silently behind her.

'I was just wondering what this trip is going to be like.'

'Fifty-fifty – work and sightseeing I expect. Why, don't you want to go?' he asked, looking surprised.

Pip suddenly saw out of the corner of her eye that Jim Parrish was heading in their direction, and it reminded her of earlier events that day. Should she mention her supposed pulled muscle to Andy? No, somehow she didn't want to tell lies to him. But she had to do something quickly, before Jim was upon them.

'I'm just not feeling on top form today, that's all. I'll be OK before next week though,' she said and dived into the water, leaving hardly a ripple on the surface. If there was one thing she was sure of, it was her skill at diving.

Jim and the stopwatch kept them all hard at work

for the next hour, with only one welcome break in all that time. Her team-mates were putting their all into this practice session but gradually Pip found that her concentration was waning, and her performance suffered.

Once they were all out of the water and towel-draped, Jim usually made little comments and gave helpful hints where they were needed. When it came to Pip he looked her up and down with a slight frown on his face.

'Would you mind bringing me my clipboard, please? I left it on the bench over there.'

Pip was surprised but did as she was asked. However, she did wonder when he called after her, 'Hurry up!'

No one but a fool would hurry along the wet edge of a swimming pool and she was already moving as fast as she felt was safe. What was the matter with the man? she thought, feeling vaguely irritated. With clipboard in hand she returned and was met by his professional assessment.

'No indication of tension, strain or muscle spasm that I can see. Your mother did have a word with me about your . . . injury.'

That slight hesitation between the words might not have been noticed by anyone else, but Pip could hear it. Jim knew – she was sure he did.

'So, young lady, it's either lack of concentration or else sheer laziness. Which is it?'

Once again Pip felt that rush of resentment against such a public scolding. The fact that she had private coaching in addition to these practice sessions didn't give him the right to make her look foolish in front of all her team-mates.

31

'Neither. But I am getting rather tired of jumping through hoops like some circus animal,' she said fiercely.

'I see,' he said with a tired smile. 'Well, all I can say is that perhaps it's a case of shape-up-or-ship-out. It's up to you, Pip.'

She didn't reply, and she tried not to flounce off like a child having a temper tantrum, but the effort of controlling herself brought tears to her eyes. Then she felt a hand on her shoulder and heard Andy's voice in her ear.

'Take no notice of him, I'm sure he doesn't mean it. After all, you're one of the best he's got.'

'Thanks Andy.' She gave him a watery smile, thankful that her wet face and dripping hair obscured any tell-tale tears. 'But I'm beginning to wonder if it's all worth it.'

'Don't say anything you might regret later — just leave it for now.'

Pip decided to take Andy's advice not to react to Jim's taunts. She walked into the changing-rooms but wasn't watching where she was going and tripped over a pair of flip-flops that someone had carelessly left there. Her feet shot from under her, she hit the wall and landed awkwardly with her right arm twisted under her.

Pip yelped with pain but there was no one around to hear her, or to help her, so she struggled to her feet and stood for a moment holding on to her elbow. It really hurt yet, at the same time, it felt numb and in a panic Pip wondered if it was broken. She tried to wiggle her fingers — it wasn't easy but they did move.

Getting dressed wasn't easy either and as she tried

to push her wounded arm through the armhole she noticed that there was blood on her T-shirt. Falling against the rough brick wall had produced a wide graze which was now beginning to ooze blood. Pip dabbed at it with her hanky.

It suddenly seemed ironical that only that morning she'd been pretending to fall and hurt her leg and now she really had fallen and given her arm such a bang that it was making her feel quite sick.

'Serves me right,' she muttered. 'That was what they call "tempting fate", I suppose.'

Collecting her things, she pushed them into her bag but carried it over her left shoulder because her right one was still hurting.

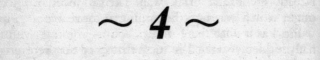

~ 4 ~

When they met up in the entrance hall, Mum noticed the blood-stained T-shirt straightaway.

'Pip, whatever have you done now? Are you all right?'

'I fell in the changing-rooms and bashed my elbow on the wall. It does hurt but it isn't broken.' Pip wiggled her fingers but by now the initial numbness was wearing off, and she winced with pain.

'Let me see,' Mum said, gently feeling Pip's wrist and moving on up the arm to the elbow, then to the shoulder. 'If you fell with your full weight on that arm it could be nasty. There are a lot of small bones in your wrist you know. You might have fractured some of them. We'd better have it checked.'

Pip had to admit that her wrist was now beginning to feel very painful but she didn't like the thought of having it 'checked', whatever that might involve.

'Don't fuss, Mum. It's OK, really it is. I just feel a bit sick, so can we go home now? Please.'

Mum put her arm around her, being careful to avoid the painful shoulder. 'I'm not fussing, love, but I really think after a fall that numbs your arm we ought to have it X-rayed . . . just in case.'

Pip knew that there was no point arguing; Mum had decided to take her to the hospital so there was nothing more to be said. Mum was probably right anyway. It was better to know for sure that nothing was broken.

They arrived at Accident and Emergency, checked in at the desk where Pip retold the story of her accident and then they were shown which coloured line to follow. It meandered around corners and up and down corridors, eventually leading them to the appointed waiting area. This seemed more like an airport lounge than a hospital waiting-room. There were comfortable easy chairs, potted plants, pictures on the walls and even a drinks machine in the corner. Several people were waiting, some looked poorly, and some looked worried and, as she gazed around, Pip realised that she was the youngest there.

'Are you still feeling sickly?' Mum asked.

Pip shook her head. 'Not really, that's worn off a bit but my arm is stiffening up now.'

'Well you mustn't worry, an X-ray is only like having your photo taken,' Mum said with a bright smile.

'I know that, but how long are we going to have to sit here?' Pip said impatiently. 'It's well past tea-time already.'

Her mother's eyes opened wide, then she began rooting about in her handbag for her purse. 'Oh dear, I'd forgotten your father. I should go and phone him.

He'll be wondering what's happened to us. You don't mind if I leave you and find the public phones, do you?'

'I'll be fine, Mum. They were in the entrance, on the right as we came in.'

Her mother had only just disappeared around the corner when from the other direction came the sound of voices and laughter. In through the archway came a white-coated male nurse pushing a boy in a wheel-chair. The boy was dressed in jeans and a T-shirt and he was wearing a baseball cap on his head.

'I see you later?' said the boy.

'Not tonight, Jean-Luc. I'm off duty in ten minutes,' said the nurse.

Jean-Luc waved as the nurse departed, then looked around the waiting area. Seeing someone his own age, he positioned his wheelchair near to where Pip was sitting and then he smiled at her.

'Hello. I'm Jean-Luc. Are you on your own?'

His direct approach was unexpected but Pip couldn't help responding to his warm smile.

'Call me Pip,' she said cheerfully. 'And I'm not really on my own, *Mother's* gone to phone home.'

'Who is at home?' he asked.

'A hungry dad with no tea,' she answered with a grin.

He pulled a funny face and rubbed his stomach.

Pip had to laugh, he looked so comical; then she found several thoughts going through her mind at once. He must be ill or he wouldn't be in a wheelchair – and yet he seemed so relaxed and happy compared with most of the other people in the waiting area. He and the nurse were obviously old friends so, presumably, he'd had a long stay in hospital already. She wondered why he was here and what was the matter with him.

Then Jean-Luc got out of the wheelchair, went over to the drinks machine and got himself a coffee. 'Do you want one?' he called to her.

'No, thank you,' she replied.

By now Pip was really curious – why the wheelchair if he could walk? She found that she was staring at him and, as he walked back, he seemed to read the question that was in her mind – and he answered it.

'Yes, I can walk but I soon feel tired – because of my treatment – so I'm given a wheelchair.' Then with that same directness and complete lack of embarrassment he continued, 'Why are you here? You look well.'

Pip listened to his slightly foreign accent, probably French she thought, and she stared back at his cheerful grinning face. She didn't feel offended. After all, she'd been wondering the same things about him, the only difference was that he'd spoken his question aloud.

'I could say the same thing about you. You look too cheerful to be a patient here.'

With a quick gesture he lifted off the baseball cap, revealing his almost bald head, hairless except for a downy fluff that looked like the bloom on a peach. Then he replaced the cap and gave her a sidelong glance.

'It's warmer with it on. I've had chemotherapy.'

For a moment Pip didn't know what to do. She felt that she should say something but she didn't know how to express it. His treatment was probably for cancer and she'd heard that the side effects of chemotherapy were often quite unpleasant. This boy must be very brave to be so cheerful after all he had

37

been through.

At last, and almost in a whisper she said, 'But you're so happy.'

'That's because I get better every day. Also I have a very good friend who gives me courage.'

'The nurse who wheeled you in?'

Jean-Luc laughed. 'Oh no, though he is my friend of course. But no, the special friend I mean is Jesu.'

Pip found herself staring at him in surprise. It wasn't the sort of thing people usually said, at least – not amongst her friends. And yet, there was something refreshing and natural about the way he'd spoken of Jesus as his friend.

'You call him Jesu,' she said quietly.

'Yes, in France we do. Here you give his name an extra letter – but he is the same one.'

'That's true, the same one in whatever language.' Pip looked across at him and noticed that his expression had changed. He looked thoughtful too, even a little sad.

'I miss going to my usual church,' he said wistfully but almost at once his smile returned. 'But there is a small chapel here in the hospital. It is inter . . . something.'

'Interdenominational,' Pip put in helpfully.

'That is probably the word I look for,' he agreed. Then, changing the subject, he continued, 'You still have not told me why you are here.'

'It's a long story really but I'm only here to have an X-ray – this arm, wrist and elbow,' Pip told him, lifting her right arm as she spoke.

The pain was still there and she winced, then she began to tell him all about her fall at the baths. She was going to tell him about her pretend fall down the

38

stairs at school when suddenly she stopped in mid-conversation. Mum was back and she couldn't let her mother hear that.

'I'll tell you some other time perhaps,' she half-whispered. He understood and gave her a wink.

Mum's arrival happened to coincide with the arrival of a nurse who went up to Jean-Luc, said, 'They are ready for you now,' and began to wheel him away.

They barely had time to say goodbye to each other before Jean-Luc was removed from the waiting area, and the last thing Pip remembered him saying over his shoulder was, 'Good luck with your X-ray!'

When her turn finally came, and after the X-rays had been checked, Pip and her mum agreed that she had been very lucky indeed. There were no bones broken, only severe bruising.

As they drove home Mum asked, 'Who was the boy in the wheelchair? Do you know him?'

'Not really, he just came up and started talking to me. I think he's been very poorly.'

Pip was just going to tell her mum that he was getting better and that she thought he was from France when Mum interrupted.

'I meant to ask you earlier – what was Jim saying to you at the pool-side? I could see you through the café window but I couldn't hear.'

Pip felt a sudden surge of annoyance. She'd asked about the boy in hospital but hadn't been interested enough to listen to Pip's reply. All Mum ever seemed concerned about was the swimming, as if nothing else mattered in life except thrashing through the water at speed. Clenching her teeth, Pip refused to answer.

'Was it about the muscle strain in your leg?'

And that was another annoyance on Pip's list. While they were in the X-ray department, Mum had insisted on telling the radiographer about her daughter's fall down the school stairs, until Pip eventually half-admitted that it was more of a stumble than a real fall. Mum had raised her eyebrows at *that* admission.

'Were you pulling back with your crawl? Or was your leg really hurting this afternoon?' Mum continued relentlessly.

Still Pip said nothing.

'Pip, are you listening?'

This was too much and Pip felt her anger rising – at her mum for fussing, at Jim for threatening to remove her from the team and at herself for getting into such a ridiculous situation.

'Oh shut up, Mum!' she snapped. 'I'm too tired to think straight and I'm sick of the whole thing.'

Instead of being cross at Pip's rude outburst her mother patted her knee consolingly. 'Yes, of course love. You've had quite a day what with one thing and another,' she said sympathetically.

In bed that night, Pip's thoughts took quite an unexpected turn. She thought about the stupid mess she'd got herself into. If Jim really did carry out his threat and remove her from the team . . . what a disgrace it would be, both for herself and for her parents.

With a sudden wave of remorse she realised that she'd be letting Grandpa down too – Grandpa who had taught her to swim, encouraged her and delighted in each success she'd had over the years. She felt ashamed of herself and inwardly resolved to try and recover her lost enthusiasm. It would be hard but she knew that she must try – and she'd have to tell Natalie.

On the following day Natalie soon noticed how awkwardly Pip was holding her arm and thought it was all part of the plan.

'That's a good one. You can't swim with a stiff arm.'

Pip smiled rather sadly. 'Things have changed since yesterday. I really have hurt my arm,' she said. Then she told Natalie what had happened – but for some reason, that wasn't even clear in her own mind, Pip left out the part about her meeting with Jean-Luc.

She also began to tell her friend of the decision she'd made in bed the night before, but Natalie was only half-listening. Instead she was bursting to tell Pip all about the first meeting of Computer Club and she launched into a long rambling account that Pip could hardly follow. Natalie was using words and initials that meant nothing to her, and the one time Pip had ventured to ask a question, Natalie's answer left her none the wiser.

'I thought you'd have known that already. RAM stands for Random Access Memory,' Natalie had said.

'Oh, I see,' Pip said quickly, but really she hadn't a clue what that meant either. Just knowing what initials stood for didn't mean that she understood. To her a ram had curved horns and said 'ba-aa', and the picture that this conjured up – of a small, woolly animal head-butting around inside the computer – made her chuckle.

'I don't know what you find so funny. I thought you'd be pleased about that.'

'Yes, I am – really,' Pip said, suddenly conscious of the fact that she'd missed a whole chunk of Natalie's story, but hardly liking to admit it.

'That's OK with you, is it? So you'll try to get to the next meeting?'

'I think so – I mean, I hope so – well, you know.' Pip's floundering response made Natalie raise her eyebrows.

'Sometimes I wonder about you. Are you going to be with us or not?'

Pip didn't bother to reply but just laughed and picked up her bulging bag, pushing the escaping banana firmly back between the books.

At that moment the sound of the buzzer made further speech impossible anyway, and the two girls went into school together.

During the next week, Pip's arm improved rapidly. She kept to her decision and even found swimming practice quite an amusing challenge when Jim presented her with two plastic float-boards that the babies used. He'd connected them together to make a sort of floating splint for her painful arm, and she found that his idea worked very well.

On the last day before half-term, nobody was in any mood to work – neither staff nor pupils – and there was already an atmosphere of winding-down in the air. The Lost Property Box was trundled out and disgorged a motley assortment of unlikely objects, some to be claimed and others disowned out of embarrassment.

'Whoever would bring a thing like that into school?' someone whispered as Mrs Fisher picked up a small stuffed snake and held it up for everyone in the assembly hall to see.

At break, people were standing around in groups talking about their own plans for half-term holiday; some heading for far-away places with strange sounding names, others staying at home.

'Are you going somewhere nice?'

It was Lorraine, a girl from the Special Maths group. Pip had the impression that all she really wanted was an excuse to talk about her own forthcoming holiday, which was bound to be somewhere exotic. Pip didn't feel like going into long complicated details about the swimming trip.

'I'm going on a mystery tour,' she said, making her voice sound as mysterious as she could. After all, it was partly true since she wasn't exactly sure where the coach would be stopping.

Lorraine looked at her for a moment, said, 'Oh how lovely,' in a very insincere way and then moved away.

Natalie winked at Pip. 'She'll be off to bend someone else's ear now because you didn't play the game, did you? You were supposed to ask her where *she* was going.'

'I don't want to know where she's going,' Pip replied.

Natalie had already said that she and her two cousins were spending a few days walking in the Lake District and Pip had told Natalie the full story of her week ahead. She also remarked that she was almost certain Andy would be going.

Natalie had heard Andy's name mentioned several times before and it seemed that he loomed large on Pip's horizon. She gave her friend a broad grin and said, 'Nudge, nudge, wink, wink, say-no-more!'

'Don't be silly, he's just one of the team,' Pip said.

To which comment Natalie replied, 'Oh I believe you!'

Something in Natalie's voice made Pip want to

move the conversation on to safer ground, so she said the first thing that came into her head.

'Did I tell you about a French boy I met at the hospital?'

Natalie looked at her in surprise, 'No, you didn't. Tell me *more!*'

With impish mischievousness Pip decided to make her friend wait.

'I can't now, I'm late for class already. I'll tell you after half-term.'

~ 5 ~

The alarm went off soon after six and Dad came upstairs with mugs of tea to rouse Mum and Pip. They had to be up early this Saturday morning.

'The birds aren't even awake yet, Dad,' Pip mumbled and turned over again.

'Oh yes they are, and I'm here to shake you out of your nest,' he said, bumping the edge of her bed with his knees.

She reached for the tea and sat up, blinking sleepily. Fortunately, both she and Mum had done their packing the night before, so all they had to do was have a shower each, grab a bite of breakfast and then get down to the bus station before seven-thirty.

While Pip was slipping on her dressing-gown, after her shower, she noticed the aroma of frying bacon gradually beginning to creep upstairs. She wondered if she could face a cooked meal so early in the morning.

'You must eat something,' Mum said when they were all downstairs. 'It'll be a long time before the coach stops somewhere for lunch.'

The egg, bacon and tomato seemed to look up from her plate and give her a greasy stare as she prodded them about with her fork. Pip made a brave attempt and managed to eat most of it.

Dad had the car in the drive and their two suitcases already on board by the time Pip came outside, and she climbed into the back seat quickly. But not quickly enough. Mum was just closing the front door.

'What are you wearing?' Mum said, horrified. 'I thought we'd agreed on your little brown dress.'

'It makes me look fat. Besides, I feel more comfortable in jeans and I bet most of the others are wearing jeans anyway.'

'Do you always have to look like all the others?'

'Why not? What's wrong with them?'

'Nothing, I suppose.'

Dad, always the peacemaker, intervened before it developed into a real argument, and his calm voice smoothed the troubled waters. 'Well I always think you look very nice in your jeans, Philippa, and at least they won't get creased on a long journey, will they?'

Mum looked down at her thin jersey-wool dress in dusky-pink and with one hand she ironed out a small crinkle before she got into the passenger seat.

'Come on, Matthew, it's time we were off,' she said.

The coach was only about half-full when they arrived at the bus station and, while Dad saw to the luggage, Mum and Pip chose their seats. The twins, Marietta and Daniel, were sitting across the aisle with Mrs Roscoe sitting behind them on her own.

Looking out of the window, Pip could see Andy talking to someone – a girl – and she knew that he didn't have a sister. She pursed her lips and turned away just in time to see Mrs Hemingway getting into the coach. Andy soon followed her and they sat together at the front. Pip saw that the girl was waving but Andy took no notice and she wondered why, but then firmly reminded herself that it was none of her business anyway. Several more cheerful faces said 'hello' and Pip returned the greeting, noting that she had been right – most of them were in jeans.

The coach filled up, they said goodbye to Dad – pressing hand patterns against the cold glass window – and at last the swimming team began its journey.

Pip soon decided that motorway travel was always boring; miles and miles of ribbon-road, built-up grass banking and the hissing swish of vehicles passing in the fast lane.

For a while she and Mum checked the itinerary sheets and talked about what they expected to be doing in their free time. After that they played magnetic chess but that didn't last very long; staring down at small black and white squares on a board that vibrated in rhythm with the coach's movement soon gave Mum a headache. So she put her head back and went to sleep while Pip read her book. Lost within its pages she was transported into another world.

In what seemed like no time at all, they were off the motorway and winding along minor roads towards the place where they'd be stopping for lunch.

The River Restaurant was exactly as the name suggested; a low wooden structure built on the bank of the river and surrounded by trees and flowers, with picnic tables set out on the close-cropped grass. Sunlight through the trees dappled the area with dancing shadows and the chuckle of the river, swirling over and around small boulders, sounded cool and refreshing on a hot day.

The three Roscoes came and joined Pip and her mother at their table, unloading plates of salad and bottles of fizzy drinks. Pip discovered how hungry she really was and demolished her baked potato and tuna, leaving her plate clean.

The twins soon left the table to go down to the water's edge and Mum and Mrs Roscoe went back inside for cups of coffee, leaving Pip to guard the handbags. Idly she broke the crust off the last piece of bread and began tossing small pieces to the sparrows.

'It's not good for them – bread.' Andy had wandered over to keep her company.

'But everyone tosses bread for the birds,' she retorted.

'Yes, but everyone shouldn't – it clogs up their innards. In the wild you don't find bird bakers baking bread for their customers, do you?' He leant across her, retrieved the fatty rind of the ham which Marietta had left on the edge of her plate, and threw it on to the grass a little way off.

Two sparrows fought for it, taking an end each, and the tug-of-war that followed made Andy and Pip laugh.

'And how many pork butchers do you find in the wild, Andy?' she said, giving him a sarcastic nudge.

He grinned. 'True, but they think it's a worm.'

She looked up at him, standing with one foot up on the bench where she was sitting, and into her mind flashed the scene she'd witnessed at the bus station. Before she knew it the words were out of her mouth.

'Who was that who saw you off this morning?'

He gave her a quizzical glance but replied, 'Oh, you

48

mean Trudi. She wanted a lift into town – shopping or something.' He paused then added, 'She's my cousin.'

Pip was aware of a sense of relief – which surprised her. She recalled Natalie's comment the other day, 'nudge, nudge, wink, wink, say-no-more', and wondered if perhaps Natalie knew more about her than she knew herself.

'She looked really nice, I thought,' Pip said hastily, hoping to cover up her slight embarrassment.

'She's a pain in the neck,' he said with feeling. 'Never stops talking. Once she starts it takes a crowbar to break into the conversation.'

Pip grinned and made a mental note not to chatter and rabbit on when Andy was around. The return of the two mothers with their coffees brought the conversation to a close, and Andy departed, saying that he'd see her later.

The village of Halton-under-Weal was another two and a half hours' journey and, when the coach pulled up in the village square, Pip and her mother discovered that their bed for the next two nights was to be at the Elsinore Guest-House.

This rather grand and imposing name actually belonged to a very small cottage – hidden away up a steep street just outside the village centre – but the room was comfortable and little Mrs Amptil seemed very eager to offer a first class service. An evening meal promised for seven o'clock left them plenty of time for tea and cakes first and then a wander round the district afterwards.

On the way into the village, Mum thought she'd spotted a church with a Norman tower. Mum enjoyed visiting little old churches and Pip always associated holidays with such visits.

Inside, the church was cool and there was a distinct smell of 'oldness' – a mixture of wood polish, brass cleaner, flowers and dusty kneelers. With half her mind Pip was listening to what her mother was telling her about the building, but the other half of her was listening to the silence and peacefulness which was so strong that you could almost touch it. Sunlight through the narrow windows brought shafts of brilliance into the nave where she was standing, and Pip watched little dust particles flickering up and down.

Pip found herself thinking of Grandpa again. This church was so like the one in Ballantyne where he'd always taken her when she'd gone to visit her grandparents' house. Perhaps it was the big brass eagle lectern in front of her now that had triggered the memory so clearly. Grandpa used to say that if you loved someone you showed it by the way you lived and the things you did. As a small girl she'd thought that polishing an eagle with metal polish was a funny way of showing that you loved Jesus, but over the years she'd understood what had motivated Grandpa to express his feelings in such a practical way. Being a military man, a well-pressed uniform and shiny brass buttons were second nature to him, and so keeping the church brass bright and sparkling was a way of honouring God's house. Some people had thought old Mr Rhodes was rather stern and unbending but Pip knew him better than that. He could be strict sometimes but he was a warm, loving person underneath.

As she thought about him, she could almost imagine that she saw him sitting in one of the pews, looking at her. She smiled to herself . . . But would he approve of the way she behaved sometimes? Did the things she had been doing show what she was like underneath the surface? Perhaps they did. Perhaps she was a mixed-up muddle of a person who didn't know what she really wanted and was short-tempered with people who loved her. Yes, she really was making a bit of a mess of her life at the moment and she knew that would have to change.

Pip linked arms with her mother and looked sideways at her. 'I'm sorry if I've been a bit grumpy lately.'

'What brought that on?' her mum asked with a smile.

'Just thoughts running around in my head,' she replied.

When they came out of the church there was no one around. It was amazing how quickly a coachload of people could vanish from sight, even in such a small village. The coach itself was tucked away in the car park behind the hotel where several families were staying, and the rest of the people had been absorbed into guest-houses.

The other guests at the Elsinore were Gary Briggs and his mother, who didn't appear except briefly for the evening meal.

After breakfast next morning, everyone gathered outside the village hall and waited for the coach to pick them up. They were heading for the Leisure Centre at Allington where, Jim Parrish told them, they would find one of the most up-to-date facilities in the county. When they arrived they were met by the manager of the complex, a very cheerful man who welcomed them and showed them around. Two of the dads and one or two of the mums asked questions and seemed very impressed with the answers.

Pip was not impressed. She hated the chrome turn-stiles, which were like tip-tilted spiders, that prodded you in the backside if you didn't move through fast enough. She didn't appreciate having to cram her clothes into a basket no bigger than a deep fat fryer which you then thrust into a hole in the wall, where an attendant 'filed' it away. In return she was given a red plastic, numbered disc suspended on a rubber band.

'Loop it around your straps,' Marietta suggested.

'Yuk, how tatty. I much prefer our old Lido where you can trust folk and leave your stuff about.'

They moved through a fine mist-spray and a shallow trough which smelt of pine disinfectant. Daniel was capering around on the edge of the pool and seeing his sister he shouted out to her.

'What were yours like? I think I've just been through a vat of sheep dip.' He laughed and took a racing dive into the water.

The Allington girls' team was already in the water doing a warm-up session so Pip stood for a moment or two looking them over, surveying the competition and trying to assess who would be the ones to watch when it came to time-trials. She could see that Andy was doing precisely the same thing, leaning non-chalantly against the diving gantry, surveying the male opposition. He gave her a grin and a wink and she returned the signal.

This pool was nothing like the one at home. Instead it was T-shaped – the long leg of the 'T' divided into lanes with the top of the 'T' as the deepest area, nearly eight metres, and the diving platform at one end. At the other end of the T-cross, where Pip happened to be standing, were three holes spaced well apart forming a triangle. She felt at them with the tip of her big toe and discovered that they were obviously to receive something with a screw-thread.

One of the Allington team answered Pip's unspoken question. She was a tall, slim girl with very close-cropped hair.

'It takes a carrying seat for the disabled; it swings out over the water and lowers them in.'

'Are they safe? I mean, do they stay in the seat or can they swim alone?' Pip asked.

'Some of them can swim by themselves. The water supports them and even a small movement gets them going.'

'I think that's wonderful,' Pip said slowly. Looking down at her own strong, well-muscled legs she realised – with an intensity that almost took her breath away – just how fortunate she was.

'Wonderful,' she said again.

'It is, isn't it?' said the girl with a smile.

They didn't exchange names or continue the conversation, they simply acknowledged each other as fellow swimmers and then each returned to their own group of friends. But for Pip it had been a very moving experience and it provided her with the impetus she had been lacking recently. Her whole outlook to today's time-trials altered. She no longer saw the Allington team as competitors, to be beaten for the mere sake of winning, but instead it was to be a celebration of the skill and enjoyment of swimming. It was a celebration of the freedom to move, and move with ease through the medium of water – and of the inner will channelled through a body that was fine-tuned toward that end.

One by one the swimmers, both from Allington and from Jim's visiting team, worked off the various heats – the crawl, the backstroke, the butterfly and the medley. This time, Pip was putting every ounce of her energy and training into the operation; willing herself to be as near perfect as possible; urging herself forward with that renewed sense of purpose that had been triggered by her experience earlier in the morning.

Sadly, when she came out of the water at the end of her third attempt for best-of-three, she could tell that she was still not fast enough – nothing like fast enough.

'I tried. I really tried,' she said wearily. 'I pushed myself till it hurt.'

Mum patted her shoulder encouragingly. 'I know you did, love. Put your robe on and sit here a moment while I get us some hot chocolate from the machine.'

The towelling robe enclosed her in its soft warmth and she sat on the pale-green wooden benching with her knees drawn up to her chin, her arms hugging them in a childlike comfort gesture.

When Mum returned with the steaming poly-styrene cups they sat together in silence for a while.

'Look at that girl over there,' Mum said. 'The one with the mauve swimsuit. I've been watching her all morning.'

'I talked to her earlier,' Pip replied, remembering that conversation very clearly.

'She's fast – and so are the other two that she's with.'

'Yes, they're good,' Pip admitted.

'Take a closer look at them. What do you notice particularly?'

Pip sipped her drink and stared through the rising steam. 'They're tallish – they've both got blonde hair, almost white in fact.'

'No, more than that. Look again,' Mum prompted.

'Oh – you mean how short their hair is?' Pip said at last.

'Exactly. They've got it almost like that Olympic swimmer used to be. No resistance, the water just streamed past his head.'

This raised a faint smile from Pip. 'Streamlined is OK I suppose, but he was as bald as an egg. No way, Mum!'

'I'm not suggesting you go bald,' Mum said. 'Although who was that girl in the *Star Trek* movie? She was beautiful.'

Nesting her empty cup inside her mother's on the bench she unlooped the rubber band and let her two wet plaits swing down to below shoulder level.

'I think I'll go and get changed now,' she said, moving away.

Changing took no time at all, but it always did take twice as long as anybody else to get her hair even reasonably dry. She stood near the power point in the wall and, with the diffuser trained on her cloud of golden hair, she had time to consider her mother's remarks. Always having to bring her own hairdryer with her was just one more thing to remember, and it was even more of a nuisance finding that some pools didn't even have a power point in their changing-rooms. Would it be so bad after all to have it cut a little shorter? She bunched her partially dry hair into a coil and secured it with an ethnic leather disc held in place by a wooden pin.

As she came out of the changing-rooms, she could see that Jim was talking to Mum. Too far away to hear what they were saying, Pip's only clue lay in their body language: Jim was smiling and the lines of his body were relaxed. He leant forward slightly as if imparting some pearl of wisdom. Mum, on the other hand, seemed tense and a little anxious; her rapid hand movements and twisting of the head adding to the impression of unease.

Pip's soft sandals made no noise as she walked carefully along behind the tiers of seating. It wasn't that she meant to creep up on them but she couldn't help wondering what was being said. What she did hear left her feeling cold . . .

'Perhaps you're too good a cook, Mrs Johnson. She's beginning to bulge in all the wrong places for a swimmer.'

His voice was not unkind, merely jovial and Mum replied in the same vein. 'She's a growing girl.'

'Yes, indeed,' he said. Then noticing Pip standing at the end of the row of seating watching him, he added, 'Hello, we were just talking about you.'

Pip bit her lip and said nothing – she was still reeling from the shock of what she'd just overheard. How could he discuss her shape as if she was a prize animal at a cattle show?

He was still smiling at her. 'I thought you put on a good showing Pip, well done. Now we must try to—'

She didn't give him time to say more.

'To *slim*?' she said, staring at him with suppressed anger. 'Yes, I *heard*.' She turned and walked away but out of the corner of her eye she saw her mother hold up her hands in an attitude of helplessness.

Pip found their coach in the parking area and persuaded the driver to open the door for her. She'd had enough. All her recent enthusiasm had evaporated leaving a void which made her feel desperately tired and beaten. With just those few words Jim had killed something, undermined her self-confidence and made her feel sick inside. What was the use of him saying 'well done' to her face and 'too bulgy for a swimmer' behind her back?

For the second time in as many days she changed her mind about her swimming. She'd lost it, that edge that she'd once had, that keenness to be there in the lead. What did it matter anyway?

'Why should I bother?' she announced to an empty coach.

The driver was too busy with his newspaper to hear her.

Pip slumped down in her seat and stared out through the coach window at the dark-green of a holly bush. Her own face reflected in the glass took her by surprise – it was a sulky, sullen face with a downturned mouth, and it looked so ugly glaring back at her. What frightened her even more was how suddenly her moods changed from being happy to being angry and then to being depressed. It had only been the other day, when she was in the church with her mum, that she'd vowed to herself to make a change and get herself sorted out. And yet she'd broken that resolution so soon. Even though she hadn't actually said anything rude to Jim, what she'd thought in her head would have made him furious; and thoughts were sometimes just as destructive as words.

As she sat there thinking, once again she remembered Grandpa and how he'd said, 'If you have a problem and can't help yourself, just ask Jesus to help you solve it.'

It had sounded easy when Grandpa said it, but could she really ask Jesus to stop her behaving like a fool? Well, maybe she'd give it a try next time and see if it worked.

Nothing was said about the incident for the rest of that day. Pip and Mum skirted around the issue and talked of other things, just inconsequential mother-and-daughter chatter. But something hung heavy in the air between them. They both felt it.

In the morning they left the Elsinore Guest-House behind them and the next venue was a town in the East Midlands somewhere. Now Pip wasn't interested enough even to ask the name of the town. It was busy, bustling and the air was heavy with diesel fumes and this time Pip and her mother were in an hotel right in the town centre.

The decor was predictable: a lot of brass fittings, dark wood and maroon plush furniture and drapes. The food was good and Pip stuck a perpetual smile on her face, was friendly to everybody and kept her own thoughts well under cover. This went on until nearly bed-time and at last Mum decided that she'd have to do something to bring them back together. The gap between them was just too uncomfortable.

'Philippa, I've been thinking – it's a while since you had a new swimsuit, and here we are with a free day tomorrow and all these lovely shops. Would you like that – a shopping spree? We could both get one or two bits and bobs.'

'Yes, Mum, that would be nice. I do need a couple of new T-shirts.'

Mum relaxed on one of the twin beds and smiled

across at her.

'We could also go to Gaston Maurice – I'm sure he's got a salon here – because if we're going to have something done with your hair it needs to be well cut. What do you think? About your hair I mean.'

Pip put down the magazine she'd been leafing through and gave her mother a long thoughtful look. Was this the time to test Grandpa's advice? Was it right to ask for God's help about such little personal things? Yes, it might be. Pip sent out a very short prayer-thought: please Jesus, help me not to lose my temper.

Obviously Mum still believed in her as a swimmer and was trying her best to be positive. Perhaps short hair and a new swimsuit might even help turn the tide for her. Personally she doubted it but there was no harm in trying. Involuntarily one hand moved up and touched the thick waves of hair – it would feel strange to be without it.

'OK, I suppose. And then I could say you'd finally driven me hairless!' She smiled cheerfully as she said it and Mum didn't even notice the slight hint of sarcasm in her voice.

'Now, about this new swimsuit,' Mum went on. 'Mrs Peterson was saying that she'd got Mandy's new one a size smaller than she usually takes – that way it sort of . . . flattens her out a bit in front.' Mum gave a nervous little laugh. 'You know – less water resistance that way.'

'Oh Mum, most girls my age want to stick out in front, not be squashed flat!'

'Well yes, I know, but it'll be only while you're swimming.'

'Thanks for those few words of comfort.' Pip

laughed, got up from the chair where she'd been sitting and went over to the two twin beds. She put her arms around her mother and gave her a big hug.

It was good not to be at cross purposes any more; she hadn't liked the strained atmosphere of the past few hours but she'd been trapped within her own cloud of anger and unhappiness. But the cloud had passed. It must have been that simple little prayer that had done it.

'If you think it'll work, I'll give it a try,' she said.

'That's my girl,' her mother said.

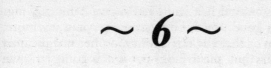

~ *6* ~

The swimsuit was really quite flattering, as well as being flattening. It was midnight-blue with a silver stripe from her right shoulder across to the top of her left thigh, and it felt as close as a second skin.

At Maison Maurice they were given an appointment for later in the afternoon. It wasn't Gaston himself but despite that the hairdresser exuded style and confidence.

Once seated, Pip tried to steel her mind against the trauma of what was to come. In fact, she shut her eyes rather than witness the increasing spread of golden hair that carpeted the floor around her chair. She began to wonder just what instructions Mum had given to this silent stylist with the flying scissors. She tried to ask but his only response was a noise like a chattering squirrel – a kind of 'tut-tut' through his teeth. Pip left it at that, wondering wickedly if he had a broad Midlands accent and this strange avoidance of speech was simply to hide the fact that he was about as French as Jack Duckworth or cucumber sandwiches!

The moment Pip saw herself in the mirror she knew instantly that it had been an *awful* mistake. She shouldn't have let Mum persuade her into having it cut – not as short as this anyway! In her imagination she'd built up a picture of how it was going to look – neat and cool like a rock star. The reality was nothing like that. As she twisted her head for a better view in the hand-held mirror, all she could think of was how bare and obvious her skull was under its sparse covering of hair.

'Mum, I look like a *turnip*!' she wailed.

'No you don't, it looks very smart – very stylish.'

'But there's hardly anything left, just a few tufts. I'd no idea it was going to be like this.'

'It really suits you, Philippa, honestly it does.' Mum turned to ask the hairstylist, 'Doesn't it suit her?'

What else would he do but agree anyway? Pip thought. He's the one who's carried out the evil deed so he's hardly likely to condemn his own work!

'Oh well, it'll grow back eventually I suppose,' she said, her voice heavy with resignation.

Pip looked at her mum's flushed face and suddenly felt sorry for her. She was probably about to pay a fancy price to Monsieur Maurice for this, and after all, Pip had agreed to have it done so it was partly her own fault too.

She tried to smile bravely as she said, 'I expect I'll like it once I've got over the shock. I wonder if sheep feel like this at shearing time?'

The visit to the small town baths on the following day was a vastly different experience from Allington Leisure Centre, and they were told that these baths were soon to close down in favour of a new complex in the suburbs. The place was old, white-tiled and had rows of little cubicles along two walls. Each had a wooden door that squeaked when you pushed it, two hooks to hang your clothes on and a slatted wooden board to stand on. The smell of chlorine was so strong that you could taste it and Pip wrinkled her nose.

'That brings back memories,' Mum said, pointing to a notice that read, 'Deep End 7 feet'. 'We didn't think in terms of metres in my day.'

Pip grinned. 'Yes, I suppose the whole place has a sort of old-world charm.'

'Less of your cheek and go and get changed,' her mother ordered with a smile.

Since all Jim's team were making their way separately from their various hotels, no one except Marietta and Daniel had yet seen Pip's new hairstyle. At breakfast time Daniel hadn't even noticed. Marietta's comment was, 'You've had your hair cut.'

Mrs Roscoe only said, 'Very nice dear,' rather vaguely.

Pip came out of the cubicle feeling self-conscious. The swimsuit was fine and, though it compressed her somewhat in places, it was no tighter than Mandy's. What Pip wasn't looking forward to was the reaction to her turnip-head.

A great many thoughts flitted through Pip's mind in the space of a few seconds and she found herself monitoring them. How many people were like Daniel – and wouldn't be aware of any change? How many would state the obvious?

How many would be insincerely polite? And how many, or how few, would really think she looked nice? Did she really care what people thought anyway? Better get it over with, she decided, striding across to the quaintly labelled 'Plunge' area.

Emerging from one of the doors on the far side were Andy and Tim. Now that more people had arrived there was so little room that they were sharing, two to a cubicle.

Pip stood statue-still and waited. Andy did a double take and then he turned to Tim, made some remark that she could only guess at, and both boys were laughing as they moved towards her.

Pip felt as though someone had punched her in the stomach. Obviously she did care what people thought – or certainly what one person thought of her. All she wanted to do was to run away somewhere and vanish from sight; hide her unsightly haircut; hide her head in the sand like an ostrich until her hair grew back again. She felt so miserable and helpless all of a sudden and there was no one she could talk to.

Andy was within a few feet of her. She didn't want to look at him, not now. More than that, she didn't want him to look at her. Before their eyes met, she turned away abruptly and dived into the water.

She avoided Andy for the rest of that day . . . for the rest of the tour, in fact.

Half-term was behind them, now it was back to school and a whole new set of jibes, jokes and comments to survive. Pip was on the defensive the moment she walked through the school gates and she gave a good tongue lashing to anyone who dared even to mention the dreaded haircut.

'Give it a rest, Pip,' Natalie said at last. 'You've bitten everybody's head off, so what do you do for an encore?'

'Well, can't you hear them? That bunch from Year Ten – they're laughing behind my back. I'm fed up with it.'

'So am I. You're getting paranoid about your hair. Don't be so sensitive. I've told you umpteen times that *I* like it, in fact I'm seriously thinking of having mine cut now I've seen yours.'

'Really?'

'Yes, really. Now can we change the subject?'

Natalie ruffled her friend's hair playfully and then ducked for cover as Pip tried to grab her by the wrist.

After that, Pip tried to calm down and had almost succeeded by the time the buzzer went for break. Then suddenly she heard a voice behind her say, 'Who's that?' followed by his friend's voice replying, 'You know who – looks like a boy, swims like a fish . . . it has to be Pippa – or is it Flipper?'

That was the last straw. She whipped round, faced her teasers and glared at them eyeball to eyeball. 'You slimy *little* toads, you *pathetic* apology for human beings. Get out of my way!'

Pip elbowed them aside roughly and stormed off towards the vending machines on a lower corridor. She'd been going to get a packet of peanuts anyway but when she saw all the bars of chocolate and bags of various potato products, something inside her snapped. Emptying out her pockets and delving into the deeper recesses of her bag she collected up quite a healthy sum of money – and spent the lot. Dropping coin after coin into the slot she didn't try to make a selection, instead she bought one of everything that looked chock-full of calories.

With her bag now bursting she headed for the

tennis courts, prised open the door of the racket store and settled herself amidst a pile of old rubber mats and tennis nets. They chafed her legs but she didn't care. She didn't care about anybody or anything; she didn't even care what she looked like any more. Jim Parrish thought she 'bulged in all the wrong places' didn't he? Well, she'd show him *bulges* all right . . . bulges in every place. With something like perverse delight, she tore the wrappers off the chocolate bars and thrust them into her mouth.

The buzzer went but she ignored its shrill demand to go back to lessons. She just sat there nursing her hurt pride and eating solidly until there was nothing left to eat.

Pip stayed in the racket store all morning, getting more and more bored. She picked up a racket, found a moth-eaten old ball and played a one-sided game of tennis against the wall but even that began to pall.

'So, what have I proved?' She tossed the question into the air and hit it with an answer. '*Nothing*. And what am I?' she queried again. 'A silly ass who's stuffed as full as a pig.'

Pip sank back amongst the mats and tennis nets and groaned inwardly. Why was it that she could never do anything right? She'd lost her temper again and all that it had achieved was to make her feel upset – the boys hadn't cared – they'd just laughed at her and walked away. Anyway, they weren't the problem – it was Pip herself who was the problem. 'I don't want to keep blowing my top,' she moaned. 'Please help me to chill out.'

As she was talking aloud in the quietness of the racket store, she suddenly had the most curious thought. She was alone here and yet what she'd just said was a cry for help – and it sounded almost like a prayer. That raised an even more curious thought: would Jesus understand words like 'chill out'? Then she remembered Jean-Luc talking about Jesus; obviously he would understand French words, wouldn't he?

Remembering the easy, natural way Jean-Luc talked about his friendship with Jesus brought Pip's thoughts to a sudden standstill. What must it be like to have such a close relationship that you could call him a friend? She might use words like wonderful and divine but they made Jesus a figure in the distance. The word 'friend' made him seem so much warmer and closer.

She sat quite still for a moment. She wished she could feel like that.

Pip looked at her watch. Ten minutes to lunch-time. The very thought of going into the school canteen and facing food made her feel distinctly queasy. So queasy in fact that she picked up her bag, and all the tell-tale chocolate wrappers, and hurried across the tennis courts. Once back inside the school building, she felt even worse and rushed to the nearest toilet block, arriving only just in time. She was violently sick.

Laura Maitland, who'd only been in school half a year, heard someone being sick and felt sure she ought to tell someone, so she rushed out and told the first teacher she met. Miss Rathbone followed Laura into the toilet block expecting to find something really serious.

Pip remained behind the locked door but Miss Rathbone was insistent.

'Who is in there?'

Pip couldn't help herself and was sick again, but

afterwards she reluctantly gave her name and emerged looking pale and shaken.

'Ah, Philippa Johnson – yes, you should have been in my room last period, shouldn't you?'

Pip nodded, suddenly realising that Laura's intervention, rather than being a nuisance, had almost been a stroke of luck. Part of the unofficial 'pupils' code' was 'never tell a teacher anything they don't need to know', but Laura was a new girl and didn't know any better. However, in this case the girl had actually done Pip a favour. Far from being in trouble for missing class, Pip found herself being given care and attention. Apparently there was a 'bug' going around the area and others had been sick.

Almost before she knew what was happening, Pip found herself on a chair outside the deputy head's room and, with the door being slightly open, she heard Mrs Cardew talking on the phone. The words 'virus infection' and 'incubation' were used and from that it seemed obvious who was on the other end of the line.

Meanwhile, Natalie had been searching everywhere for her friend, with no success. It was only when Mrs Johnson arrived at school some twenty minutes later that Natalie heard half of the story – Mrs Johnson's half. So she hung around in the entrance hall waiting for Pip and her mother to come through.

'What's happened to you?' she asked, looking worried.

'I've been sick – tummy bug,' Pip said, but chose her moment to give her friend an exaggerated wink.

'How are you feeling now?'

'Awful.' Unnoticed by all except Natalie, Pip managed their thumbs up signal. The message got through but it would need a phone call to make events clearer.

By the time she got home, Pip wasn't quite sure how she felt. Physically she was fine once the cause of her sickness had been removed, but she couldn't admit to being really hungry so soon, and eyed the neat soldiers of dry toast with some distaste. On the plus side, she'd already got half a day off school and if she played her cards right she might manage Tuesday and Wednesday off as well.

She took the phone call from Natalie on the extension so that she was free to talk, and when Natalie heard the account of the feast in the racket store she laughed until she was helpless.

'You're a prize prat, you are! Fancy paying good money for chocolate bars and then losing the lot.'

'That bit I didn't intend. I just wanted to . . . get back at them.'

'You certainly did that. Actually there's a name for it – they call it comfort eating – but your result doesn't sound very comfortable to me.'

'Well, I'm definitely not going to swimming practice this week. I've decided to play this up for all it's worth.'

'We don't want you getting a chill on your tum, do we?' Natalie said, entering into the spirit of things.

'Too right. I'll stay home and chill out for a bit,' Pip said laughing.

By Thursday, Pip decided that it was time to 'feel a lot better' – if for no other reason than to get a square meal. Mum had given her little helpings of bland food and Pip yearned to get her teeth into something solid again.

At school people asked after her health and seemed not to be noticing her hair at all – it hadn't even been a nine-day-wonder, just two-and-a-half days.

The rest of the week passed. She spent part of the weekend down at Natalie's and by Tuesday Pip found herself in a strangely unsettled mood. It was as though something was hanging over her – threatening to drop – and at odd moments during the day she caught herself wondering what it was that she didn't want to think about. Then she remembered – it was Andy. She didn't want to have to see that look on his face – laughing at her – laughing at her hair.

However long would it take for her hair to grow? Even a little longer would help. Now when the water flattened it, her head would look like a cannon ball moving along the pool, and she didn't want him to see her like that. Natalie agreed that if she felt as strongly as that about it she might as well try the 'sickness game' again.

On Wednesday morning she waited until after the first lesson and then said that she felt very sick. The toilet block wasn't the nicest of places to spend time but, since Pip wasn't really sick, she dragged a chair in from the corridor, propped her feet up on a wash-basin and read her magazine for half an hour. Then Natalie came rushing in.

'I think you'd better prepare yourself for the worst,' she gasped. 'Mrs Cardew is on her way down.'

Natalie disappeared behind a convenient door and Pip had just hidden the magazine and arranged herself in the chair like a drooping flower, when in walked Mrs Cardew.

'Are you feeling any better?' she enquired.

'Not really. Perhaps I haven't got rid of the bug.'

Mrs Cardew gave her a searching look and there was an expression behind her eyes that Pip couldn't quite read. Was it concern or disbelief? Pip hoped she wasn't going to ask if she'd actually been sick because it wouldn't be possible to meet that gaze and tell a blatant lie. Fortunately Mrs Cardew didn't ask.

'Come up to my room,' she said quietly. 'I have something for you.'

Pip followed her meekly, already having a shrewd suspicion what lay ahead. Out came the dreaded brown bottle and a large spoon. She couldn't do other than open her mouth and take her medicine.

'If you're ill . . . there's nothing quite as effective as kaolin and morphine for settling the stomach,' Mrs Cardew said with a smile.

There was just something a little too pointed about those words 'if you're ill'. Pip knew she wouldn't be able to pull that stunt again at school.

However, she didn't go to swimming practice that evening.

~ 7 ~

Pip and Natalie had been planning this outing for some time; a sunny Saturday had been all they were waiting for. Now a sandwich box, two bags of crisps, a couple of apples and a bottle of lemonade were soon assembled for their afternoon on the river. Perhaps 'river' was too exaggerated a name for the brook that meandered past the end of the Johnsons' garden and away down the valley.

Pip unlocked the shed and together she and Natalie lifted the small fibreglass skiff and carried it down to the water's edge. It was a chubby little white boat with two bench seats and a pair of oars slotted into their rowlocks, and although it wasn't built for winning any races, Pip managed to get quite a speed out of it when it was her turn to row.

'Let me have a go,' Natalie said.

Changing seats in mid-stream was a minor disaster as one oar fell out from its thole-pin and began to float away. The water was only knee-high, if that, so

Pip pushed up her jeans and stepped out of the boat in pursuit of the wayward oar. She soon captured it when it became entangled in a clump of water-weed.

'Hold on to it this time,' she said, climbing back in. This action made the boat tip dangerously to one side but it righted itself as Pip placed her weight centrally. In her haste to regain the oar, Pip had forgotten to remove her trainers, which were now soggy and dripping into the bottom of the boat.

'Clever,' said Natalie with a grin.

'Never mind me. You concentrate on your rowing – you're forever catching a crab.'

'I'm what?'

'Not digging it in deep enough. Your left oar keeps scudding out of the water and drenching me with spray.'

'Sorry, I'm sure!'

Natalie soon got the hang of it however, and they moved out into deeper water again, steering down-stream and towards their destination.

At last they came to a sort of island – a long thin spit of land which had built up where the water swirled around a curve. They grounded on the fine pebbled sand and, taking an end each, lifted the boat well clear of the water. A muddy area showed evidence of many duck feet but there was no sign of the birds themselves. Natalie carried the tartan rug and spread it out on the grass higher up, while Pip followed with the picnic things.

'I love it here,' she said, laying out her wet trainers to dry in the sun and taking the offered sandwich.

'Anything to do with water seems to have a mag-netic attraction for you,' her friend replied with a grin.

'I didn't mean that. I meant being on an island

where no one can get to you.'

'Unless they have a boat too.'

For a while they lay in the sunshine munching crisps and talking about desert islands and what they'd take with them.

Eventually Natalie said, 'Pip, tell me something. What's suddenly changed with you and swimming? You used to be mad keen.'

Pip went on plaiting together three grass stalks, her fingers going through the motions deftly − out of habit. She recalled all too vividly the sight of her long hair lying abandoned on the hairdresser's floor.

'People change,' she mused. 'Things that were once important seem to fade out of focus and you see . . . other things instead.'

'You mean things like Andy Hemingway?'

'No I don't,' Pip said sharply. 'And don't mention him − I want to put what happened right out of my mind.'

'OK if that's the way you want it, but you can talk to me. I *am* your friend after all.'

'Sorry, I didn't mean to snap at you. It's just that I'm in what Grandpa used to call a 'cleft stick' − caught like those bits of weed there.' Pip pointed to a forked stick embedded in the bank. A clump of water-weed was caught in the cleft where it had wedged firmly, and at the same time it was being swirled this way and that by the force of the water.

Gradually, as she tried to explain her confused feelings to Natalie, she began to see things more clearly herself. She knew that she was changing but her parents either couldn't *see* that, or else couldn't *accept* it. So, she was torn between 'doing her own thing' and hurting her parents; or doing what they expected of her and suffering in silence, feeling wretched. She was pulled first this way and then that, swirled about like the trapped water-weed and held firmly by the love of her family.

'Why don't you talk to them like you've been talking to me?' Natalie suggested. 'Come straight out with it and don't beat about the bush.'

Pip smiled wistfully. 'Grandpa was the only one I could really talk straight to – and now he's gone. I do try to talk to Mum and Dad but it gets me nowhere. Dad listens but I always feel that I'm taking up his valuable time; that he's expecting a client to phone or he's thinking about something else that's a world away from what I'm saying.'

'How about your mum?'

'The same but different. She listens but she doesn't hear me. She thinks she already knows everything about me but, just because she's been there ever since I was a baby, it doesn't mean that she knows what I'm going to do from now on.'

'You've got a problem then, haven't you?'

Pip nodded and stared down at her toes. Funny things, toes. It brought back a memory of Grandpa when he'd been teaching her how to improve her jack-knife dive. He suggested that after the springboard jump, and when at her highest point, she should think of inspecting her toes – touching them briefly with her finger ends before straightening out to enter the water. It produced the almost perfect position for that dive, and Pip still used Grandpa's little mind-picture. It was such a small thing in itself but, as he'd always told her, it was attention to detail that was the mark of the perfectionist. That's what he'd always wanted her to be – a perfectionist – a world class swimmer; and that was what Mum and Dad wanted for her too.

Pip gave a deep sigh.

Her friend looked up. 'That came from a long way down. What's the matter?'

'I was just remembering Grandpa and the things he used to say.'

'Like what?'

'Well, like doing everything to the best of your ability, even the little things. He said that even when you think no one is watching you, you owe it to yourself to do your best and that God is always ready to help you.'

Natalie said nothing for a moment or two, then she put on a rather sheepish grin. 'Oops – that's a thought that brings me up with a jerk. I'm afraid I don't live up to that ideal at all.'

'That's just it, neither do I. I can't any more. I mean . . . I know inside myself that I'll never be a county class swimmer, so what's the point of fooling myself? I'd rather not do it at all than do it badly, but I can't say that to Mum and Dad.'

'Why not, if that's the truth?'

'I don't know . . . just because . . . I suppose because it would be such a disappointment to them. I'd be letting them down somehow.'

'Rubbish,' said Natalie forcefully. 'Surely they'd rather have you happy than famous? I thought we'd already agreed that it was time you made a stand and told them how you feel. Have you changed your mind again?'

Pip put her hand up to her temple – a little mannerism she always used when she felt ill at ease. Now, of course, there was no longer the thick hair to run her fingers through. Instead her searching fingers found only a short cropped stubble. This was sufficient reminder of the way events had been moving lately; and 'no' to Natalie's question – she hadn't changed her mind again. She was going to find some way of putting her point across and since talking hadn't worked with Mum and Dad, she'd just have to find some other way.

'No, no change of mind about the swimming. But I just know they won't *listen* to me . . . Have you had any other bright ideas?'

They talked cheerfully as they packed the picnic things and re-launched the boat. On the way home they jokingly came up with a variety of wild ideas which they knew full well would never work, but Pip found she was deriving a perverse sense of amusement from plotting even such impossible schemes to avoid swimming practice on Wednesday nights.

It wasn't until late that evening that Pip stumbled upon a plan of action by herself. She noticed it in the bathroom cabinet when she was doing her teeth – a packet of laxative chocolate. The whole bar taken on a Tuesday, she thought, should produce an effect that would keep her out of the water on Wednesday evening. It was only another short-term plan but it would do nicely for this week. She'd certainly not be forced into swimming practice whilst in the grip of *that* little complaint.

Tuesday morning came and Pip set her plan in motion, solemnly munching her way through the chocolate laxative. All might have been well if it hadn't been for the fact that the school canteen had plums and custard on the menu that day, and Pip had a particularly large helping since it was one of her favourites. The cumulative effect was devastating and hit her in all its fury almost as soon as the buzzer went for lessons. Pip asked permission to leave the classroom – not once but again and again and again. Red-faced with embarrassment and breathless from the necessary speed of these repeated exits, Pip began to feel exhausted – and rather foolish.

'What's your rush?' Natalie said, on one of these hasty exits.

'I'll explain later,' her friend replied in a low voice.

Once back in the classroom, and sitting in the seat Natalie had saved for her, Pip was on the point of whispering the sad tale but Mr Brennan prevented this by fixing the two girls with his relentless stare. It seemed that he hardly took his eyes off them for the remainder of the lesson.

At last, however, Natalie did manage to whisper, 'Are you OK?'

Pip shook her head and mouthed something about 'the runs' but Natalie got entirely the wrong message, wrote something on a scrap of paper and slipped it to Pip.

The note read:
Cross country runs aren't until next week.

Pip gave up, shrugged her shoulders and managed to remain in her seat for the further ten minutes which brought the lesson to a close. Then she scrambled for the door and fled.

When at last the two girls had the time and opportunity, Pip told the sad tale of her latest attempt to get out of swimming practice.

'What an *air-head*! Laxatives! And *whatever* possessed you to eat all those plums as well? Didn't you know

78

they had the same effect?' Natalie asked.

Pip shook her head.

Natalie continued, 'Well, with a dose like you've had, I'm surprised you're still standing – never mind swimming!' she laughed.

'It's not funny,' Pip replied, downcast.

Natalie drew her hand down across her face in an exaggerated gesture of wiping-the-smile-off-her-face. 'I'm not laughing at you really, but you must admit, it has its funny side.'

Her suffering friend managed a weak smile but silently reflected that, once again, what she'd brought upon herself was far worse than the swimming she was avoiding. In addition to which, none of her antics had brought her any nearer to the original idea of joining Computer Club.

'This is all very well,' she said petulantly, 'but here I am putting myself through all this and it's not giving me the result I want *anyway*.'

Natalie looked at her again, all humour gone this time. 'I know, it isn't fair, is it? You know when you dashed out at the end of last lesson? Well, Mr Brennan was wanting a word with you; he wanted to know if you are still interested in joining the club.'

'What did you tell him?'

'I said – yes, you were, but you'd had a run of bad luck recently.'

Even Pip couldn't help but laugh this time. 'You can say that again!'

'No pun intended,' Natalie giggled.

~ 8 ~

'You are coming home with me today, aren't you?'
Natalie said, collecting her things together and stuffing
them into her bag. 'Even if Mum is out, we can find
ourselves a snack to eat.'

'Yes, and then we can look through those newspaper cuttings you were telling me about.'

Weeks beforehand Pip had undertaken to write an
article for the school magazine, but time was ticking
by and the deadline was approaching. It was Natalie
who had suggested that Pip should write about something with local flavour, and she'd mentioned that her
dad kept a file of 'local interest' press cuttings.

Natalie found her key, opened the front door and
she and Pip went inside. There was no sound and no
welcoming greeting, so Natalie threw her bag down
on the table in the hall, nearly knocking over the
carefully arranged display of grasses, dried flowers and
berries. Instinctively Pip put out her hand to steady
the container. Natalie threw her jacket over the newel

post and bounded upstairs, taking them two at a time.

'I'll not be a minute!' she called over the banisters.
'Get yourself a drink if you want one. They're in the
fridge.'

Pip wandered into the kitchen. She'd been to
Natalie's many times before but each time there
seemed to be something new or different to see. This
time there was the dried flower display on the hall
table, obviously the result of Mrs Orwell's night-school
classes on flower arranging. In the kitchen, she found
another addition to the family – a large and very
lifelike pottery hen sitting on a pile of shiny glazed
eggs. Cautiously she lifted the hen by its cold feathered
head and found that the whole bird-lid lifted off,
revealing a clutch of real eggs underneath.

'I see you've found Henrietta,' Natalie said with a
chuckle. 'Mum bought her from this place in Wales.
I can't remember its name but they made that TV
series *The Prisoner* there.'

'You mean Portmeirion,' Pip said. 'Yes, we've been
there too. It's a strange place but I liked it.'

'Well, you would. It takes one to know one.'

With a grin Natalie reached across and switched on
the radio then, raising her voice above the sudden
eruption of sound, she asked, 'Are you hungry? I am.
How about beans on toast?'

Pip agreed then looked about to see if there was
anything she could do to help. There wasn't. Natalie
was doing it all, whizzing around the kitchen opening
cupboards and clattering cutlery drawers like a mini
whirlwind, so Pip opened the fridge and got out two
ring-pull cans for them. She stood looking out of the
window and it was then that she saw something she
didn't expect. From the kitchen window there was a

clear view of the garage along the far side of the garden, and it was just possible to see in through the small garage window. Pip could see quite plainly the reflection of something red.

'Your mum's car is red, isn't it?'

'Yes, why?'

'Well, it's still in the garage but she's not here. Do you think she went by bus into town?'

'Hardly likely. Bus travel makes her feel queasy.'

Natalie quickly switched off the radio then without another word she disappeared upstairs, leaving Pip to watch the bronzing toast and the bubbling beans. When Natalie returned she simply said, 'I guessed as much. She's got another of her migraine headaches and she's asleep in bed with the curtains drawn – can't bear the daylight.'

'I hope she'll be better soon,' Pip said.

'Yes. She'll be fine after she wakes up.'

The two girls made as little noise as possible so as not to disturb her. They had their quick snack and then went through Mr Orwell's collection of press cuttings. It didn't take Pip very long to copy out the one or two items around which she'd be basing her article. After that they sat and talked until it was nearly time for Pip's bus. It was during this talk that an idea began to form – another ruse for breaking away from the Wednesday swimming practice.

Maths was the second period of the morning and, if she was going to set the plan in motion, now was the best time, Pip decided.

'But why in Mr Brennan's lesson?' Natalie asked.

'Because!' Pip exclaimed grinning. 'He may look stern on the outside but he's an old softie at heart.

He'll be a push-over.'

Natalie wasn't sure she agreed. 'I hope you're right,' she said quietly, more to herself than to Pip.

Every so often Pip would rub her eyes and screw them up tight until they watered, then she'd rub them some more. This ferocious treatment soon had the desired effect; her eyes were red-rimmed and watery. Only then did she get Natalie to attract Mr Brennan's attention.

'It's my friend Philippa, I don't think she's feeling very well,' Natalie said, her voice suitably charged with sympathetic emotion.

He rose to the bait like a trout to the fly, walking up between the two front rows of students' chairs and coming to a stop in front of Pip. She had one arm on the wide arm of the chair, which doubled as a desk, and the file of notes she was writing in hung precariously over the edge. When she took away the hand which had been covering her eyes, he gasped. She must have looked awful.

Before he had a chance to speak Pip said, 'It's my eyes, Mr Brennan. I can't see properly.'

'Oh dear, you certainly don't look at all well. We'd better get Miss Mumford to take a look at you.' He turned to the hovering Natalie. 'Can you help your friend down to the rest-room while I get hold of Miss Mumford?'

A terrible urge to giggle welled up inside Natalie but she firmly quashed it, since that would have given the game away immediately. It was just the picture his words conjured up that made her want to laugh. The idea of thin, gangly Mr Brennan 'getting hold of' a vast, well-muscled Miss Mumford was enough to make anybody laugh – in addition to being a physical impossibility. She looked sideways at Pip, hoping to catch her eye and share the joke but Pip had other things on her mind.

For instance, everybody in the school knew that Miss Mumford had attended an in-service course on First Aid in Schools. Pip wasn't looking forward to the Head of the PE Department 'taking a look' at her. If anyone was going to see through their latest ruse it would be Miss Mumford, but Pip comforted herself with the thought that she'd memorised the symptoms well enough to be convincing. After all, Natalie had told her in great detail of how it affected her mother, so all she had to do was to 'look sick and talk symptoms', as Natalie had put it.

Pip and Natalie arrived at the rest-room first. They'd just had time to close down the Venetian blinds when the door opened and in walked Miss Mumford, followed shortly by an anxious-looking Mr Brennan who'd come as soon as the buzzer signalled the end of the lesson.

'She can't bear the light in her eyes Miss Mumford, so I've closed the blinds,' Natalie said quickly.

'Very sensible. Thank you my dear; you can go now.'

Natalie hadn't expected to be dismissed quite so abruptly. She'd wanted to be there as moral support for Pip – and also to hear what happened. Mr Brennan was hovering kindly but helplessly in the doorway and Natalie had the distinct impression that Miss Mumford would have dismissed him too – if it hadn't been against her professional code of conduct to do so.

'Is there anything else I can do?' he enquired, giving Pip a little smile as he waited for his colleague's response.

'No thank you, Mr Brennan. I can manage now.'

Natalie stomped off registering mild annoyance; Mr Brennan wandered off in the direction of the staff-room, so Pip was left alone to face her uncertain fate at the hands of Miss Mumford. She delivered the answers to questions in a shaky but assured voice and mentioned each of the symptoms which she'd rehearsed with Natalie: beginning with the dull ache which started at the base of the skull and gradually moved forward, the flickering of peripheral vision – like a bad TV picture – and ending with the feeling of nausea that threatened to turn into actual vomiting.

Miss Mumford looked serious, tapping her lips with a crooked first finger in an attitude of concern, then she asked the final question.

'Have you had these symptoms before?'

Pip hadn't expected this query and at that moment she didn't know how to answer. If she said 'no' – then how would she have known that the nausea could turn to vomiting? On the other hand, if she answered 'yes' – this would surely mean that she already knew she was subject to migraine attacks. Pip was caught in the tissue of lies like a fly in a web, and the spider was standing there – waiting for a reply. She had to do something quickly. There was only one way out so Pip took it. Slapping her hands across her mouth she gave an almost perfect simulation of retching. Miss Mumford abandoned the questioning and instead opened the door to the small toilet which adjoined the rest-room.

'Will you be all right by yourself?' Miss Mumford asked. Pip nodded, still continuing the awful noises. 'Then I think I'd better phone and have you taken home.'

Watching Miss Mumford's retreating figure, Pip heaved a sigh of relief and clasped her hands above her head in a gesture of triumph. It was a pity Natalie wasn't around to see how expertly she'd played the migraine sufferer role.

Mum arrived looking hot and worried. Whatever Miss Mumford had said on the phone had obviously given her a nasty shock and, once again, Pip felt her conscience pricking. It really wasn't fair of her to let Mum worry over something that wasn't true, and in that moment she very nearly gave way to the promptings of her conscience. It would have been so easy to tell her mother that she wasn't ill, just pretending because she wanted time off school . . . but no, that wasn't true either. The whole thing was becoming more and more complicated. Mum would have been very annoyed, but Pip knew she deserved that. She hovered on the brink of admitting everything – but at the last moment she saw Natalie watching from behind the bike sheds as she and Mum walked towards the car park.

Things had already gone too far; there was no turning back now.

She climbed into the car and listened in a kind of daze as her mother kept repeating the same three questions: How are you feeling now? Can you hear me Philippa? Why don't you put these on? Over and over again, like a tape-loop, she asked those same three questions . . .

At last Pip snapped out of her strange state of mind and found that Mum was holding out a pair of sunglasses, to shield her eyes from the daylight. Perhaps they were a suggestion from Miss Mumford, or did Mum already know something about migraine headaches?

She accepted the glasses with a quiet, 'Thanks Mum,' and hid herself behind their reflecting mirror lenses.

The car didn't turn up Tophill Brow, instead they were heading straight into town and Pip turned to look at her mother's familiar profile; the lips were drawn into a tight line and she was biting at them anxiously.

'I want to go home, Mum.'

'I know love, and we will, but first I'm taking you to see Dr Armitage. I phoned him as soon as I heard and he said that if you were well enough he would agree to see you straightaway, without an appointment.'

Pip gasped. A cold wave of fear rippled through her, starting in the pit of her stomach and creeping up with icy fingers until it crawled across her scalp. She never enjoyed visits to the doctor or the dentist but on this occasion it was ten times worse – there was nothing the matter with her. She knew it and so would Dr Armitage. This whole idea had been a ghastly mistake and she wished with all her heart she'd never started it. What would he say to her for wasting his time like this? His precious time that should have been used seeing patients who really were ill. She felt like a fraud, like a criminal almost – and she felt so very ashamed.

Slowly the tears began to well up and overflow, trickling down behind her mirrored sunglasses. She fumbled in her pocket and found an old paper hanky to wipe the tears away. Mum didn't notice; she was too occupied in finding a parking space and ushering her daughter into the doctor's waiting-room. The place was empty because surgery was officially over until the evening, but the receptionist had heard them come in and she popped her head around the door to check.

'I phoned earlier,' Mum said.

'Yes, it's Mrs Johnson isn't it?' Then turning to Pip she said, 'Doctor Armitage will see you both now.'

Suddenly Pip realised that her mother would be there beside her, to witness her disgrace. She didn't quite know if that would make it worse or better. They knocked and waited until the lighted panel flashed 'enter'.

Dr Armitage was relatively young and quite good-looking in a languid way. As he motioned to Mum to pull up a second chair, he gave Pip a deeply searching appraisal from behind his gold-rimmed glasses.

'Hello Philippa, and how are you feeling now?'

'Terrified of discovery,' would have been the honest answer, but Pip realised that she was too far along the road to turn back so she'd have to act out this charade to the bitter end. She recited her fictitious symptoms, adding some suitable facial expressions where she felt they'd do most good – then waited for his response.

He took her temperature, looked in her eyes with his thin pencil-light and gently manipulated her head from side to side. Then he asked the same thing that Miss Mumford had asked, 'Have you had this sort of headache before?'

This time she couldn't get out of answering by pretending to retch.

'Well, sort of,' she replied, her voice barely audible.

'Perhaps you're worried about something?'

'Not really.'

'Does it happen regularly? Once every month

for instance?'

'No.'

Dr Armitage lowered his voice until it was almost a whisper and he smiled at her. 'How about just before maths lessons?' he said.

Pip felt the blood rush to her cheeks and she knew that they had turned as red as a beetroot. There was no way she could control this blushing reaction and nothing she said from now on would speak half as loudly as those glowing crimson blotches on her face. They had given the game away and she was angry with herself for her own failure. The anger only served to make her cheeks redder than ever.

Dr Armitage patted her on the shoulder and gave her a benign smile.

'Now don't get upset. I'm not saying that the pain isn't real, or that you aren't having headaches but . . .' and he turned to Mrs Johnson. '. . . I'm almost certain that it isn't a migraine.'

Mum was still looking worried. 'What is it then, doctor? What's the matter with her?'

'My preliminary diagnosis would be what we call "school stress". It's a very real complaint these days and it's on the increase.'

'You mean with the pressure of academic work and exams and so forth?' Mum asked.

'Exactly – and it can be very debilitating. My advice would be to take time out each week and find some form of relaxation.'

Again he was patting Pip's shoulder and his next comment was addressed directly to her.

'So, young lady – find something that you enjoy doing, something relaxing and healthy. How about swimming?'

Up until then Pip had been trying to keep a tight grip on the cocktail of emotions that was bubbling up from the depths of her being, but now she lost all control. It felt as if a taut rubber band inside her had at last snapped and all the pent-up energy was released in a sudden torrent of words.

'*Swimming*!' she screamed out. 'Is that the only thing anyone can think of when they look at me? Of all the trillions of things that human beings can do to relax, all you can come up with is *swimming*. I HATE swimming – do you hear me? HATE IT. OK, so it was fine when I was a kid, when Grandpa was around, that was fun. But I'm not a kid any more and it's certainly not fun now. Do it faster – more practice – keep up your speed – always badgering at me. I'm fed up with it, all of it. It doesn't mean *anything* to me *anymore*.'

In the momentary pause, Mum got up from her chair and stood with her mouth open like a goldfish. 'Philippa, control yourself,' she gasped.

Pip let out a cackle of hysterical laughter. '*Control myself* – that's just what I want to do but nobody will *let* me! You don't allow me time to do the things I *want* to do. I wanted to join Computer Club but could I? Oh no, it was on a Wednesday and Wednesday is swimming practice. There's never any time to find out if I've got "other interests" – and shall I tell you something? I'm probably the only one in Year Eleven who hasn't got a boyfriend. That may not matter to you but it does to me.'

Pip's outburst ended as rapidly as it had begun. She had exhausted herself of all anger and now what was left was acute embarrassment; just like she'd felt when she saw Andy and Tim laughing at her hair. She looked up at the doctor and gave a long shuddering sigh. 'And on top of all that, my hair's a mess.'

His eyes flicked from daughter to mother and back again and there was no trace of a smile on his face now. The girl was obviously under a great deal of stress and the mother had just as obviously been utterly unaware of the fact. But he knew them as a loving family so he was hopeful that they would talk out the problem at home now that it had finally surfaced in his surgery.

~ 9 ~

The evening meal had been rather silent, with a strained atmosphere. Pip had known that as soon as Dad got home he would be told all about her outburst in the doctor's surgery. Sure enough that was what happened. She had heard them talking together in low voices. At first Dad hadn't said anything to Pip but after they finished eating he put a hand on her shoulder and said, 'Let's go down the garden. I want to talk to you.'

Pip guessed what was coming. She shrugged her shoulders and stumped down the garden path ahead of him.

'Whatever made you behave like that? Your mother has told me all about it,' he said quietly.

'Yes well, you've only heard her side. What about my side? Nobody ever thinks about that!' she snapped back.

'It isn't a matter of sides, Philippa – we are a family and if one of us has a problem the others are there to help.'

'So – now you know my problem. I don't want any more swimming trophies, thank you very much. I'm sick and tired of being . . . pushed into it. There are other things I want to do.'

'Very well, we can come to terms with that; but that isn't your only problem and if you're honest with yourself you'll realise that.'

'I don't know what you mean by that,' she said, bending down to tug a weed out of the rose bed. Then she flung it on to the compost heap, wishing she could rubbish her angry feelings with as much ease. Of course she knew what he meant and Dad was quite right. In all honesty she knew that the problem was in her, not in the outside world. She felt her eyes fill with tears and she turned away, but not before Dad had seen them.

'How about starting by apologising to your mother?' he said.

She nodded and gave him a watery smile, then walked up the path and went in by the French windows. Mum was in the kitchen starting the washing-up so Pip picked up a tea towel and came alongside her mother at the sink.

'Mum, I'm sorry. I let you down. I don't know quite what happened but I just couldn't help it – it simply boiled out of me.'

Pip began drying the cutlery and placing all the knives together, then the forks, and the spoons, in neat groups on the kitchen table. It was almost as if neatness with this physical task would in some way compensate for the disorder inside her head.

'I should be saying sorry too, love. I was horrified when I heard what you said, but only because it made me realise how unseeing I'd been. I had no idea you felt like that about your swimming.'

When Dad walked in with the last of the dirty plates he heard the end of the conversation. 'Are you two still worrying about this afternoon's affair? Let it go, it's past. What we must do now is look forward, not back.'

Pip was grateful that between them they'd broken through into a new possible future and yet she was still sad at the way it had happened. She had made a fool of herself and embarrassed her mother in front of the doctor and that was not good. Dad was right; they now had to work out a new set of family guidelines to live by; guidelines which she could agree with and not just conform to. And never again would she lie to anyone about feeling ill when she wasn't. That was too serious.

When the washing-up was finished, all three of them perched on tall kitchen stools and had a Family Forum. Pip explained that she realised how much they had given up so that she could have the best coaching, but she knew she wasn't good enough to be a county class swimmer. One of her problems had been that she was frightened of failing and being a disappointment to them.

'You could never be a disappointment to us,' Dad said.

'We love you just as you are,' Mum added, giving Pip a hug.

'And then there's Grandpa – he always had such high hopes for me. I remember him telling me the parable about the man who buried his talents instead of using them. He used to say that I had a talent for swimming.'

Mum gave a sad little smile. Thinking about him was a mixture of pleasure and pain at having lost him. 'Yes, but he wouldn't have wanted you to be unhappy. I know that.'

The final triumph of the evening went to Dad. Not only did he whole-heartedly support her joining the computer club but he also let Pip know that the offer of her own PC/word processor was still available if she wanted it.

Friday morning assembly was definitely different. As the shuffling lines moved down the hall and the squeaking of chair legs ceased, Natalie nudged Pip and pointed to the platform where two extra chairs had been placed, centre stage.

'Visitors. I wonder who this time?'

They didn't have to wonder for very long. The headmaster and the two deputy heads walked to their places followed by Mr Fox, the French teacher, and his two guests. Pip immediately recognised one of the visitors. It was Jean-Luc, the boy she'd met that day in the hospital, and presumably the tall dark-haired man with the thin-line moustache was his father; they looked alike.

She bent over and whispered to Natalie, 'I know him. He's the one I was going to tell you about.'

'Mmm, he looks cool,' Natalie said appreciatively.

Jean-Luc was wearing standard gear – baggy pants, T-shirt, trainers and a baseball cap. Natalie raised her eyebrows and Pip grinned back. She guessed what her friend would be thinking: that none of their boys would have dared walk into school with a cap still on his head. But it didn't matter, guests on the platform could do what they liked; they were a different order

95

of being from lowly pupils. Besides, Pip knew why he was wearing it.

The hymn was announced and it happened to be one of Pip's favourites – 'Oh Jesus I have promised' – and she sang the words with great enthusiasm, her strong voice joining with those around her. If only she could be sure of remembering the promises that she was trying to keep – the promise not to lose her temper and snap at people, and the promise she'd made to Mum and Dad, to be a part of the family instead of being so self-centred.

As she sang, she felt hopeful and alive again; so different from the miserable feelings she'd been having lately. Mr Morris's readings from the Bible that morning included the story of the poor widow who gave all her money to God, and the theme of the assembly was that even a small gift willingly given was like a treasure.

After the final prayer, Mr Fox stood up and introduced his guests – Monsieur Dupont, who smiled warmly but remained seated, and his son Jean-Luc, who stood up a little nervously and walked to the front of the platform. Pip had to listen very carefully because Jean-Luc was softly spoken and his pronunciation of certain words was – as might be expected – very French.

He told of his earlier years in France and then of coming to live in Britain when his father and mother bought a restaurant in town. Then he began to talk about the time when he was told he had cancer and had to go into the local hospital. He said he couldn't go into too many medical details because he didn't understand them, but he did mention the word 'scanner' and 'chemotherapy' and then went on to speak of his time in the 'Children's Day Unit'. Finally he told the assembled school that now he had finished his treatment he had left many good friends behind still at the unit.

'This hospital here in our town helped me so much, and now I ask myself, "What can I do for them?" So, I come to talk to you and I am asking you please – can you help also? Can you think of ways of raising funds for the Children's Day Unit at our hospital?'

Jean-Luc stood for a moment looking down at the sea of faces reaching all the way to the back of the hall, and his question hung in the air – waiting to be answered. For a few moments there was complete silence then someone began to clap and within seconds the whole school joined in the explosion of applause. Gradually Jean-Luc's smile grew even wider and he waved happily at everyone before returning to the chair next to his father.

Mr Morris was still clapping as he turned to Jean-Luc. 'Thank you for joining us this morning and for your excellent talk. Probably many of us have questions we'd like to ask and I'm sure that between us we'll be able to find ways of responding to your appeal. Now Mr Fox, I understand you have something you'd like to say.'

Mr Fox spoke for only a few moments, saying that Monsieur and Madame Dupont had been friends of his for many years. After that he got down to practical details: during the morning and afternoon each class would have the chance to talk either to Jean-Luc or to his father. One of them would be going round the Block A classrooms and the other around Block B. 'So, if there's anything you want to ask them you'll have ample opportunity. And let's all help Jean-Luc to make his appeal a great success.'

People slowly filed out of the hall and spread throughout the school like streams of liquid. Halfway along the corridor toward Block A Natalie suddenly found her voice again. She wasn't usually so quiet but today's assembly had struck a poignant chord – she had a cousin who'd had cancer.

'That was powerful,' she said slowly. 'There was something about that boy that made us listen – and I don't just mean his foreign accent.'

'I know what you mean. It's probably because he was talking about an experience he has been through, not just something he read or heard about,' Pip replied.

'Where did you say you met him?' Natalie asked.

'In the hospital, when I went about my arm.'

'But that was ages ago! Why didn't you tell me about him before now? Anyway, I think he's really something special and I wonder what we can do to help? I'd really like to work for his appeal.'

'So would I, but I'm still a bit confused as to what the money is actually for. I mean, some items of equipment must cost *thousands* – we could never collect that amount.'

Natalie wagged a finger in front of Pip's nose. 'Remember the widow!' she said with a smile. 'She didn't hold back although she hadn't much to give.'

Halfway through the morning there was a polite knock on the door and, after Mrs Marsh's, 'Come in,' Jean-Luc appeared round the door.

'Is it convenient?' he asked.

'Yes, of course. We're having PSE which makes your visit very apt,' Mrs Marsh said brightly.

'Excuse me? What is pey–ess–ey?'

Mrs Marsh waved an expansive arm toward the class. 'Tell him, someone,' she prompted.

A voice explained the initials, 'Personal and Social Education.'

Someone else called out, 'It's really about yourself and your relation to the community – things like that.'

'Ah yes, I see. That is what I am talking about too, is it not?' said Jean–Luc very seriously.

This room didn't have desks. It was a venue for social gathering, and it had an abundance of chairs scattered about on its hard-wearing carpet. The group of chairs nearest to the door happened to have one spare and Natalie and Pip were part of that group. Pip smiled at Jean–Luc and beckoned to him.

'May I sit here?' Jean–Luc said.

'Sure. Park it.' Mark's invitation was well meant, if a trifle basic, and Jean–Luc sat down.

Suddenly he looked more closely at Pip, raised his eyebrows and asked, 'Is it you, Pip?'

'Yes, it's the same me – different hair.' Pip laughed and ran her fingers through her abbreviated hairstyle, making it stick up in little spiky tufts.

'But still I recognise you. Did you like my hairstyle so much you decided to copy?' he said with a laugh. 'We are like brother and sister now yours is cut and mine is growing back.'

At this Natalie made a funny little noise and Pip wondered if perhaps it was intended to remind Pip that Natalie wanted to be included in the conversation.

So Pip said, 'This is my friend Natalie,' and then went on to introduce each of the others in the group.

At first the questions were slow in coming but before long several other people had dragged their chairs across and were joining in.

'You can ask me things I did not tell you,' Jean-Luc offered. 'So much I did not say at your assembly because . . . I was scared of you.'

He laughed and raised both hands in a very Gallic gesture. He had nice teeth, Pip noticed – white and evenly spaced and they made his smile seem even more pronounced.

'You didn't look scared,' Pip assured him.

'Fancy being scared of *us* . . . after all you've been through. To me that seems much more scary,' Natalie said.

His expression changed at once and he turned sideways to look Natalie full in the face. 'No, you are right, but it is a different sort of scared. Some things you cannot back away from. My treatment was something I had to do, I had no choice. But standing in front of you this morning, I chose it, I put my own head in the little knot, yes?'

Everybody laughed at the face he pulled.

'Noose,' somebody said, but it didn't matter about using the right word, Jean-Luc had got his meaning across. Jean-Luc was very clever at getting his meaning across, and even more so now that he was part of a small group.

At one point Pip did ask about the vast sums of money needed for specialised equipment and it was then that he explained more about the Children's Day Unit.

The Unit was part of the hospital but not strictly in the medical sense; instead it was more like a recuperation centre for those who'd had treatment but were still weak. There was a need for games, toys and play materials and, for the children who came in on a day-to-day basis, there was the provision of meals for them and their parents. Some of the facility was hospital funded but the greater part of the money came from donations.

'Do they have a computer?' Natalie asked.

'Oh yes, there are two; one for serious work and another one in the room for . . . *le bébé.*'

'For the babies?' someone said in surprise.

'No, how do you say? For the little ones. They have the squeaking games – *Super Mario* and so on.'

Mark grunted. He was sitting next to Pip and she heard him mutter, 'Babies huh! *I've* got *Super Mario.*'

Natalie had launched into an idea that had suddenly occurred to her and she'd gone to join a group who were sitting at the other side of the room. Before long they beckoned Jean-Luc to join them. For a while Pip felt rather left out because she could see that the group Natalie was talking to were mostly her friends from Computer Club. Then she suddenly realised that there was no need to feel left out; she was free to become one of the computer club group as well now. She walked across and stood behind Natalie's chair listening to the conversation, but they seemed to be talking another language almost – words she'd never heard before – and she must have looked really puzzled because Jean-Luc looked across at her and he winked. Natalie saw him wink and turned round to see Pip behind her.

'What do you think, Pip?'

'I didn't really hear,' she said, not wanting to admit that she hadn't understood 'computer-speak'.

Later Natalie told her that in information technology class they were going to ask if they could work on programming some computer games which could be sold. The proceeds could then go to Jean-Luc's appeal.

When they were on their own together, Pip had a chance to tell her friend about everything that had happened within the last twenty-four hours. She told her about the awful visit to the doctor and her outburst when she'd at last been able to make her mum understand how she felt. She went on to tell her about the long talk she and her parents had last evening which had helped them to see each other's position.

Natalie was wide-eyed. 'Wow, and all that has happened since I watched you and your mum walking out of school yesterday. *Fantastic!*'

'I feel like a new me,' Pip said with a broad grin on her face. 'As if a huge weight had dropped away, now that I've finally decided to sort my life out.'

'Yes, I thought this morning in assembly that you seemed quite cheerful, but I never expected all this.'

'And it means I can come to Computer Club on Wednesdays, although—'

'Great, we can certainly use you. These games we're going to produce are going to take a lot of work.'

Pip sighed. 'But I know hardly anything and I've missed out on all those weeks.'

'Don't worry, a few hours "intensive" from Mr Brennan and you'll be fine,' Natalie assured her.

Pip wandered into the canteen and made a leisurely selection from the salad bar, picked up her tray and made her way to her favourite table, the one by the small window. Natalie hadn't appeared yet but she'd said she might be late so Pip started her meal. Glancing up she saw that Alan Walters had just walked in with Jean-Luc and, after he had shown the guest where to go, Alan dashed out again.

Jean-Luc collected his food then stood looking around at the several full tables and even more empty ones. Catching sight of Pip he headed in her direction.

'I shall join you? Alan doesn't eat lunch. He plays football.'

'Yes of course, sit down.'

Pip felt a momentary flutter of nervousness. What would they talk about? It seemed such a long time ago – that conversation in the hospital. She hadn't found it difficult to talk to him then, so why was she feeling anxious now? What had changed she wondered? And was there a subtle change in him too? In the way he approached her? She decided that new relationships can be exciting but also rather difficult.

As it happened she had no problem guiding the conversation. Jean-Luc took over that responsibility without any hesitation. Taking off his baseball cap and placing it on the chair beside him, he revealed an inch growth of almost chestnut-coloured hair.

'*Mon père* – he says I look like a bottle brush.'

Pip chuckled, 'Just a bit perhaps. You used to look like what's-his-name that used to be on the *Crystal Maze*. I liked him.'

'Thank you – for the compliment. I'm so glad that you like him.'

Pip wasn't quite sure if he was making fun of her or not. He seemed to have an amused expression on his face.

'Sometimes a person's hair changes when it grows again,' he explained. 'From straight to curly or the other way round.'

'And which were you before?'

'I was straight, so maybe soon I shall look like a water-dog . . . a poodle?' he said.

'I'm a bit of a water-dog myself,' she said quietly and then began to tell him about why she'd lost her hair.

He listened intently as she poured out the long story of her parents, and her grandfather's hopes for her as a swimmer, although she had already told him some of the same things when they'd met before. Then she told him of how she'd watched her long plait falling in pieces on the hairdresser's floor. It must have been because he was such a good listener that she found herself telling him so much, and all the time she was talking he met her gaze; nodding, smiling or frowning slightly in sympathy with what he was hearing. At last her flow of words dried up and she felt somewhat foolish for having monopolised the conversation for so long.

'I'm sorry I went on so much,' she said.

Jean-Luc looked at her very carefully for a few moments and then he said, 'I think your hair looks very good for you. It was nice long – but no – short hair is best for your face.'

Pip felt the colour rising into her cheeks. Why was she blushing? And why did she feel so much happier? Was it only because Jean-Luc had such a lovely warming smile?

'I have been watching you waving your arms as you talk,' he said solemnly. 'So I am guessing the X-ray showed no breaks?'

'That's right, no breaks but I had some nasty bruises. They're fading now.' She held out her arm for him to see.

'Good – then we are both healing well,' he said.

A wave of embarrassment washed over her. She had thought how much better he looked when he'd first stepped out on to the platform, and yet something had stopped her even from asking him, 'How are you?' when they'd talked. She'd wanted to ask about his health but there was the fear that he might be worse, and she wouldn't have known how to cope with that.

'I'm glad . . . you are better,' she said haltingly.

He gave her a very knowing smile. 'I know. I also think you were frightened to ask, weren't you?'

She just nodded.

'People are often like that. Illness is not all bad, you know; it has taught me a lot about understanding other people – and – sorting out what is important in this life.'

'Oh Jean-Luc, stop it. You'll make me cry . . . and I'd hate that.'

'There is nothing wrong with tears, they often wash away all the rubbish inside us,' he said and he watched for the smile on Pip's face to widen.

Quite suddenly a thought dropped into her mind, almost like a jigsaw piece that had been missing, it fitted exactly into place and completed the picture. She knew what she wanted to do and, better still, she knew how to do it.

'Jean-Luc, I've had an idea – for your appeal. I can set up a sponsored swim,' she said with excitement in her voice.

He leant across the table and laughter lines creased the corner of his mouth. 'To swim is your special talent, and in the Bible we are encouraged to use our talents, yes?'

'That's what Grandpa always used to say,' Pip said leaning forward too. Then with a sigh of satisfaction she settled back in her chair. It felt so good to know what she wanted to do. Even though she could never be a world-class swimmer she could still use the skill that she had, and make it work for others.

Jean-Luc told Pip that he and his father would be in school for a couple more hours but he didn't know if he would see her again before he left.

'So please, may I have your phone number? I must call you at home,' he said. Then he added, '. . . to talk about your sponsored swim of course.'

Pip was quite sure this time that there was a mischievous twinkle in his eye as he said that.

'Yes, of course,' she replied as she handed him a page torn out of her notebook. Her telephone number was written in red – because people don't forget things that are written in red, do they?

~ *10* ~

Pip was in the shower when the phone rang and when Mum said it was for her, the first thought was: oh rats! What a time to pick! But aloud she called out, 'Tell her I'll ring her back!'

'It isn't Natalie,' Mum said, raising her voice above the sound of splashing water. 'He said you were expecting a call.'

Pip turned off the shower, scrambled into her towelling robe and emerged from the bathroom amidst a cloud of steam. 'Thanks Mum, I'll take it on the extension.'

She picked up the receiver, said a tentative, 'Hello,' and waited.

Jean-Luc's voice was quite unmistakable and Pip was a little surprised at how pleased she felt to hear from him. He had said he would phone — but then, lots of people said that, and didn't.

'Are you doing anything on Saturday morning?' he asked.

'Nothing in particular.'

'Then would you like to come with me to visit the Children's Day Unit? I thought perhaps you might like to meet the staff and some of the children your sponsored swim will be helping.'

Pip agreed that she would like that very much and so it was arranged that they should meet on Saturday at ten o'clock, in the bus station. It had only been a brief phone call – short and to the point – but it left Pip feeling that something important had happened; almost like another turning point in her life.

'Don't be silly,' she told herself firmly and continued getting dressed, but the face that looked back at her from the mirror kept smiling. After all, he had said short hair suited her.

'Who was that on the phone?' Mum asked when she came downstairs.

'Nobody special,' she said.

'So will you be seeing him then?' came the next question.

Pip felt the colour rising in her cheeks and she drew her lips into a hard line. Why were there always questions? It was nobody's business but her own who she had as a friend. Why did Mum always have to get in on the act?

'Why didn't you listen in on the downstairs phone?' she said sarcastically. 'Then you wouldn't need to ask me.'

Her mother looked really hurt. 'Oh Philippa, I'd never do a thing like that. You know I wouldn't. What's the matter? Why are you so sharp with me?'

Pip almost snapped back with what was in her mind – because you are being nosey! – but she thought better of it, suddenly remembering her promise not to lose her temper.

'Sorry, Mum. I didn't mean it,' she said, looking a bit shamefaced.

'I was only asking because I'm interested in what you do and in the friends you make.' Mum gave her daughter a sad little smile.

'I know you are. It's *me* . . . I don't know what's the matter with me sometimes. Actually it was Jean-Luc on the phone, the boy I met at the hospital. I'm seeing him on Saturday morning.'

'I remember him. That'll be nice for you both,' Mum said.

On Saturday morning she was up and breakfasted well before it was necessary, but she'd decided to take the earlier bus into town. The next bus should get in by five minutes to ten, but if it happened to be late she didn't want Jean-Luc to think she wasn't coming. Once at the bus station she had a quarter of an hour to spare so she went into the newsagent's and bought a big bag of dolly mixtures. She was going to meet a lot of little children and somehow it didn't seem right to arrive empty-handed.

At ten o'clock on the dot she saw Jean-Luc striding across the bus station entrance; she waved and they met halfway. They exchanged 'hellos' and a few brief words but he didn't seem in the mood for talking. It only took a few minutes on the local 'Hopper Bus' to get to the hospital and, once there, Jean-Luc took her through the visitors' car park and on to a long single-storey building surrounded by shrubs and a grassy area.

'You're very quiet this morning,' Pip said, feeling the need to break what she felt was fast becoming an awkward silence.

'I am sorry. Please forgive, but coming up here brings back memories – both pleasant and unpleasant.'

Of course, why hadn't she thought before she spoke? It was natural that his mind would be going back over his recent experiences. In her embarrassment Pip reacted on impulse and, thrusting the packet towards him, she said, 'Have a dolly mixture.'

It was a childlike thing to do but it helped to ease the tension. He looked from her to the packet and back again, then he let out a great bellow of laughter.

'Bonbons, the cure for all ills,' he said picking out one or two and popping them into his mouth.

'I bought them for the children. Are they allowed?'

'Oh yes, within reason,' he said, then linking arms he led her in through the swing doors. 'Come with me.'

Pip's first impression was of light and colour and fun. Cartoon characters grinned at them from the walls and Daffy Duck stood with his beak open as a rubbish bin. Everywhere there was the sound of chattering voices and of laughter, and the whole atmosphere was one of guided activity. In some ways it reminded Pip of the infant school that she'd attended, the only difference being that here the staff were nurses and most of the pupils had little bald heads with hair in various stages of growth.

Jean-Luc had removed his baseball cap and tucked it in his top pocket and Pip, with her three-inch-long hair, almost began to feel overdressed in the scalp region.

'It's just like a school,' she said.

Jean-Luc smiled. 'They try to keep the little people interested in learning, and we older ones continue with our studies on our own.'

Pip was introduced to some of the staff, given a cup of coffee and then asked if she'd like to visit the baby room while Jean-Luc went to chat with some of his old friends who were still at the unit.

The baby room was a delight: there was a walk-in dolls' house, a sand tray and a water-bath with plastic buckets and boats, and in the far corner was a quiet area where the books were kept.

As soon as Pip lowered herself on to a quarter-sized wooden chair, she found herself surrounded by eager little patients each thrusting a book at her. So she read stories and played finger-rhymes for a while before being literally dragged off by persistent little hands; some wanted her to see their paintings and others wanted her to help them with egg-box and plastic bottle constructions.

It was hard to realise that what she was seeing was only one side of the story. Pip knew from what Jean-Luc had said that there had been pain and discomfort also for these brave little children, fighting to regain their health. And yet for all that, it wasn't possible to remain sad for very long in such a happy atmosphere.

Pip asked a nurse about the dolly mixtures and it was agreed that two tiny sweets each wouldn't do any harm. Pip had almost emptied the packet when Jean-Luc arrived back in the room and stood in front of Pip with his mouth open like a baby bird. All the children laughed as Pip dropped one sweet into his mouth. And then a little boy with big brown eyes tugged at Jean-Luc's sleeve.

'You only got one. Do you want my other one?' he said, opening his hand to reveal a tiny sticky lump.

'You are a kind boy, but no – you have it,' Jean-

Luc said gently.

There was something about this scene that touched Pip very deeply. This small boy, with all the problems he must have had in his little life, knew more about being generous with his things than many adults did. Pip knew she was very near to tears. But at the same time she was glad it had happened because it made her even more determined to do whatever she could to help these children, and those who looked after them, by giving what she had to offer.

They left the unit and made their way back into town on foot. It was such a nice day that they both decided a walk would do them good.

'Are you hungry?' Jean-Luc asked suddenly. '. . . Because I am.'

Pip looked at her watch and opened her eyes in surprise. 'I'd no idea it was that time. We've been there over three hours but it didn't seem as long as that. Yes, I am getting hungry.'

'I would have liked to show you our restaurant but it is on the other side of town, so shall we find somewhere nearer?'

Pip admitted to herself that she would have liked to see his parents' restaurant but she said, 'Anywhere suits me fine. Wherever you want.'

The Coffee Pot opened its doors invitingly as they approached, and as two customers came out they were followed by a most delicious aroma. Jean-Luc steered Pip in through the door and they chose a table near the window.

The interior of the café was done in country-cottage style, with pine furniture and folk-weave curtains on brass poles. Pip gently touched the petals of the pink carnations which stood erect in the small white china vase.

'Good, they're real. I like real flowers on a table.'

Jean-Luc pursed his lips in a half-hearted attempt to look hurt. 'Would I take you somewhere with plastic flowers? Never!' he said, sounding aggrieved.

'You might. How do I know what you like? Come to think of it, I still don't really know much about you at all, do I?'

'About as much as I know about you, but that could change,' he said.

They ordered baked potatoes with a choice of fillings and a side salad each, and while they waited for it to arrive they talked about the arrangements necessary for the sponsored swim, among other things. It wasn't until the pudding course arrived that the subject had become exhausted. Jean-Luc looked down at his plate of pancakes with sugar and lemon juice, and with his spoon he carefully moved something to the edge of his plate.

'Pip,' he said thoughtfully.

She looked up and met his amused gaze. 'Yes?' she said.

'I just wondered why you call yourself a little seed?' he enquired.

Was he making fun of her or did he really not know? 'Are you being serious?'

'It's a fair question, isn't it?' he replied.

'I suppose so. Well, my real name is Philippa and that's what Mum and Dad always call me. But nearly all my friends shorten it to Pip.'

He nodded then said, 'I like the full name, not the little seed. We have it in France too, and yours is the feminine version of Philippe, isn't it? It has a good meaning, do you know?'

She shook her head.

'It means "lover of horses". Do you like horses perhaps?'

'I've never really had much to do with them. They're beautiful to watch when they're moving though,' she replied. Jean-Luc just smiled.

While they were drinking their coffee, heads together and busy talking, they didn't even notice someone standing outside the window, looking in.

Natalie had been doing a few errands for her mum and had thought to pop in to her favourite little spot for a quick toasted sandwich. However, when she saw who was inside she decided to forego it and leave Pip and Jean-Luc to themselves.

'I mustn't be a gooseberry,' she said to herself. Pity though! Jean-Luc is a good-looking friend to have dangling on your arm, she thought cheekily. Fortunately her friendship with Pip was strong enough to keep Natalie's hand off the doorknob and she walked resolutely on past the Coffee Pot.

~ 11 ~

In the days that followed Pip and Jean-Luc saw each
other quite often both after school and over the week-
ends. Sometimes they spent the time on their own
and at other times Natalie would join them.

Pip did join Computer Club and, as Natalie had
predicted, with Mr Brennan's tuition she soon made
up lost ground. One thing she did discover though,
was that her interest wasn't anything like as strong as
Natalie's, and she grudgingly admitted to herself that
her insistence on joining Computer Club had been
more in the way of a ticket to freedom than a real
desire. When she thought back to all the fuss and all
the stupid antics she'd been through over the last few
months it made her feel slightly uncomfortable.

With this new viewpoint on life she began to see
things in quite a different perspective. From turning
her thoughts away from her swimming she'd now done
a complete about-face and was once again anxious to
be back in the water; ready to use her skills for a really

worthwhile cause.

Between them Pip and Natalie busied themselves urging their friends and acquaintances into finding ways of raising funds for Jean-Luc's appeal. Within school there was a variety of different schemes afoot: there were 'bun bakes' at home and the results were sold at break-times; a 'find the treasure' map and there was a rather yukky contribution by the biology department of 'guess the number of worms in the jar'; in fact all the usual Summer Fête type of money-makers. The only difference was that this time it wasn't in aid of school funds but for the Children's Day Unit.

'How is your computer games project going?' Pip asked when Natalie came round one time.

'It's going to take quite a while to get that off the ground. There's hours of work involved, and I'm only just on the right side of understanding the technical aspects,' her friend said.

Pip knew when she was beaten. If even Natalie was finding it hard work, then what chance had she? Already Natalie was the undisputed whiz-kid when it came to computers and Mark had, somewhat reluctantly, conceded the title to her when he saw her at work on her project.

It was at that point that Pip decided to concentrate even more of her time and attention on her own project and leave computers to the real enthusiasts.

'I've been thinking,' she said. 'This sponsored swim could be made into something even bigger – other schools as well, not just ours.'

'You've still got to give your talk in assembly next week,' Natalie reminded her.

That was certainly true and Pip felt again that wave

of panic at the very thought. It would be the first time she'd ever stood up in front of the whole school – a sea of faces all looking at her.

The next time she met Jean-Luc she found herself explaining to him how she felt, and he responded by telling her how he had felt that day, when he'd come into school with his father.

'I was speaking in my second language to a crowd of strangers, in a building I'd never been in before. I was – how do you say? – turned into a stone.'

'Petrified,' Pip supplied the missing word.

'Yes indeed. But I had asked for his help and I knew that Jesu would make me able.'

Suddenly she found that Jean-Luc was giving her the answer to her problem. Why hadn't she thought of it before? Why hadn't she remembered what Grandpa had told her all those years ago? He had said that if ever she felt troubled or frightened she must ask Jesus to help her – not ask that the situation be altered but ask that she be given the strength to face it. She looked at Jean-Luc's smiling face and thought again of some of the things that he'd already had to face during his life. For her to give a talk in assembly was nothing in comparison.

Pip smiled. 'There's one thing I like about you.'

'Only one?' he said jokingly.

'No, I'm being serious. I find it so difficult to talk about my faith and what I believe. But you do it so naturally.'

She paused for a moment, then continued, 'Do you remember once when you told me that Jesus was your friend? Well, sometimes I just wish I could say the same.'

Jean-Luc's eyes twinkled. 'What I said of Jesu is true

for me and it can be true for you too – as soon as you *really* want it to be.'

'But I do want that,' she said earnestly.

He made a little gesture with his hand outstretched and fingers spread. 'Some people call out a prayer when they are in difficulties – but that is not the sort of friendship that I mean. I think it is sad that so often we forget; only turning to Jesu when we are – how you say? – backs to the wall.'

He sighed and looked away momentarily, then his eyes met hers again. 'That was so for me too, you know. I forgot . . . until I became sick. But now I've grown bigger – inside.'

Pip looked puzzled. 'Do you mean older?'

'No, I mean that my illness changed everything in my life. Different things became important. Only one thing remained the same – my friendship with Jesu – and that made me grow bigger inside. When I began to get better I knew that I must use my life in the way that he would want me to. Do you understand? It is not easy to express.'

'Jean-Luc, I do understand. You're talking about wanting to be different . . . being committed, aren't you?'

'Ah yes, that is the word – commitment. I work for him now, not for myself.'

For Pip it was as though the clouds had parted, and she now had a much clearer view of a blue sky, and its sunshine lit up the smile on her face. Jean-Luc had been watching her and saw that smile.

'You can do this too – and then you will also know Jesu as your friend.'

'I know. It's really quite exciting!' she said brightly. 'And thank you, for your part in it all.'

With all that was now in her mind it certainly was exciting; making plans for the sponsored swim, and even the thought of talking in assembly began to seem more of a challenge than something to be feared.

One evening after supper Dad looked up from the newspaper he was reading and said, 'Is there anything you'd like Mum and me to do, to help with the appeal?'

What had triggered his question was a feature in the paper advertising a printing service.

'This chap is a friend of mine,' he said, tapping the paper. 'I'm sure he'd print some sponsorship forms for you if I asked him. When are you giving your talk?'

When Pip told him Thursday was the day, he went straight for the phone. 'Better get right on to it now then.'

Mum had already suggested to some friends who lived in the next town that they might try organising a sponsored event in their area, at their swimming club.

Of course Jim Parrish had been very pleased when Pip had told him of all her new plans. He had even gone so far as to apologise for having done so much sniping at her beforehand. He said he had done it in the hope of reviving her flagging interest. So as not to hurt his feelings, Pip said, 'I'd just had so much school work, I got tired, that's all.'

It wasn't really a lie – she had got tired, but not quite in the way she was implying; but she felt quite relieved not to be at cross purposes with him any more. He proved to be a good friend now, helping Pip to make the final arrangements for the use of the Lido.

Mum met Pip and Natalie in town after school one afternoon and told them she'd had yet another offer of help towards the appeal.

'I want you to help me choose some prizes for very small children,' she said, leading them into a department store.

'All very mysterious,' Natalie said.

'Not really. You see, at church they have a Mums-and-Toddlers group, and Mrs Ford is setting up a "sponsored splash" in the shallow pool on the same day as Pip's sponsored event.'

Pip laughed. 'I think that's great. Do you mean they're sponsored to splash folk or just to be in the water?'

'Just for being there I think, and the prizes are really only to make it more fun – all of them will win a prize for something. We'll make sure of that.'

Together the three of them filled a carrier bag with little inexpensive presents of various sorts and took them away in triumph.

'Good luck tomorrow. That's in case I don't see you before you climb up on stage,' Natalie said as they parted at the bus station.

Thursday arrived – a bright morning full of sunlight and with a slight breeze fluttering the bedroom curtains as Pip opened her eyes. Her first thought was – oh dear, today's the day – but she quickly cancelled the 'oh dear' part and forcefully reminded herself that she must be positive. She *wanted* to give this talk. She wanted it to be a success, not for herself but for all those children who needed the Day Unit and she wanted this to be the first test of her new commitment. Closing her eyes she said a silent prayer asking

120

Jesus very simply, 'Make me able to do it well.'

Then a more confident Pip got up, got herself ready and went down to breakfast. Propped against her glass of orange juice was a postcard which must have arrived by first post. It was from Jean-Luc. On one side was a photo of a brilliantly plumaged kingfisher diving into the river, and on the other side the message said:

You can do it. I did !! Best Wishes.

Pip felt her cheeks going pink; she did wish she didn't blush so easily, and why blush anyway? Just because he had sent her a card – on this important morning, perhaps?

'Wasn't that kind?' Mum said. 'He must think a lot of you.'

Yes, I suppose he does, Pip thought and felt her cheeks grow even redder.

Dad's friend had risen to the occasion splendidly, delivering a fat package of sponsorship forms in plenty of time. As Pip spread them on the table at the side of the platform she sincerely hoped that most of them would be used.

Today she would be sitting at the very end of the front row, amongst the younger children, ready to mount the steps to the platform as soon as the service part of assembly was over. Pip hardly noticed them shuffling their chairs as they came in. She stood and sang the hymn, listened to the readings and closed her eyes for the prayer – but more than three-quarters of her mind was elsewhere most of that time.

The notices had been read out and after that a silence descended on the hall. With a sudden jerk of realisation Pip knew that her time had come and slowly she climbed the steps and faced the whole school.

That one second of panic lifted the moment she silently asked for help; and then Pip launched into the talk that she'd so carefully prepared.

'Do you remember that I once had very long hair and then suddenly it was all gone? Well, this morning I want to tell you about some little children who lost their hair suddenly too . . .'

Gradually Pip found the words tumbling out of her mouth so fast that she could hardly keep pace with them. She told of how Jean-Luc had taken her to meet these children, and of how brave she thought they were. She told them that her own hair had been cut off in order that she could swim faster – and that since swimming was her 'special talent' she would now be using it in order to raise money for Jean-Luc's appeal.

Finally she said, 'You don't need to be a fast swimmer to join in the sponsored swim, all you need is determination, and the more the better.

'So will you please help? Sponsorship forms are on the table, and it tells you where and when.'

Pip stood for a moment looking at everyone. She felt exhausted and yet elated at the same time. It was a good feeling and she bathed herself in it like the sunlight which streamed in through the hall windows. Then the moment was over and she scuttled down the steps and towards the table spread with the forms Dad had helped her to provide. To her happy amazement the pile was growing smaller by the minute as numerous hands reached out and took a form before leaving the hall on their way to classes. If each person who'd taken a form only managed to find a few people to sponsor them, it would still represent a very healthy addition to Jean-Luc's appeal.

'Well done!' Natalie said, giving her friend a hearty slap on the back. 'It really came across well. Good on you, sport – as my uncle in Australia would say. He swims too. Did I ever tell you about him?'

Pip shook her head. Natalie was helping to fold down the legs of the table and carry it to the under-stage storage space. '. . . Yes, and not only swim, he surfs mostly – all that sun, sand and sea.' She sighed languidly.

Pip had a sudden mental vision of shark-infested waters and *Jaws*, and she was glad her sponsored swim would be at the safe, familiar pool she knew so well.

When she got home after school she checked through all the sponsorship forms, fastened them with a large paper-clip and put them on the hall table.

Now that the sponsored swim was so near she found herself wondering what she would feel like after it was all over. It would be rather an anticlimax . . . but then, it needn't be. Surely there were other things that she could become involved with, other ways of using her swimming skills to help others? The more she thought the more certain she felt that it was important for her to help other people. Wasn't this what Jesus wanted her to do? Almost immediately she felt that the answer to that question was 'yes'.

Pip took the phone into her own room, settled herself on the end of the bed and punched in Jean-Luc's number. When he answered she began to tell him what she'd been thinking about, and why she wanted to do more than just the one-off event – the sponsored swim.

Jean-Luc began to laugh. 'Listen, this is very

strange,' he said carefully. 'Only this morning one of the customers at our restaurant asked my father if he knew of anyone who could help handicapped children learn to swim – and of course we thought of you. I was going to mention it next time I saw you; but now you have called me.'

Pip sat with the phone grasped in her hand, hardly able to believe what she was hearing. This was certainly a most unusual coincidence.

'That's fantastic,' she gasped. She added, 'But I'm not trained to teach swimming.'

'You would not be there alone. You'd be one of a group helping to support them in the water,' Jean-Luc reassured her.

'Well then, yes, of course I'll do it,' she agreed.

'I hoped you would. Goodbye now and I'll be waiting to cheer for you, at the Lido when you do your sponsored swim,' he said.

'See you the day after tomorrow,' she replied.

~ *12* ~

This was the day. This was what all the preparation had been for. Pip looked up at the wide blue banner with its yellow lettering which stretched from one side of the pool to the other. It sagged a bit in the middle where the rope had gone slack, but that didn't matter – it was what it said that mattered.

SPONSORED SWIM in aid of THE HOSPITAL
CHILDREN'S DAY UNIT

Pip smiled. She'd really made it happen – with a lot of help from her friends and family. All her old friends from the swimming team were joining in, and lots of children of all ages from her own school and from other schools were taking part also.

There would be an evening session as well, Dad had informed her, because he had rounded up several of his friends. In fact anyone who could make it from one end of the pool to the other, without putting a toe on the bottom, had been persuaded to lend their support.

Pip saw Andy walking along the side and when he saw her he waved cheerfully. All that terrible upset she'd been through about Andy and Tim laughing at her hair . . . that had been nowhere but in her own imagination apparently. As she had later found out from Tim, what they'd been laughing at was a current joke. Andy had been quite puzzled as to why Pip had so obviously avoided him for the next four weeks.

Which only goes to prove – you should never jump to conclusions, Pip thought to herself as she slid down into the water. She bobbed up again, looking along the rows of tiered seating until she found the place where Jean-Luc was sitting. She was glad he had arrived early enough to watch her.

Of the six lanes in use, Pip was positioned in the fourth and for the next two hours she and her teammates churned up and down the pool; notching up the miles; notching up the fifty pence per length that they'd undertaken to earn.

Jean-Luc didn't sit there for the whole two hours. He went to the coffee machine several times and spoke to the groups of children, giving encouragement. But he was back in his seat by the time Pip finished her stint. With a towel thrown over her shoulders she came up behind him and put two cold wet hands over his eyes.

Jean-Luc squirmed. 'I cannot possibly guess who you are,' he said.

'I thought you wouldn't!' Pip said, laughing. 'So, when are you coming to join us in the water?'

Jean-Luc shook his head sadly. 'To my shame I have to admit it. I cannot swim.'

There always seemed to be something new that she was finding out about Jean-Luc but she'd never expected this. She'd just assumed that he could swim. She stared at him. 'Not at *all*?' she asked.

'No, not a stroke.'

'Do you want to? Would you like me to teach you?' she asked, hoping he'd say yes.

'I think that would be very good, perhaps later.'

Then he looked up at her and laughed. 'Shall I shave it off again? I might have good speed with my hairless head, yes?'

'Could be, but I'd rather you kept your hair on,' she replied. 'I'm off to get dressed now. Wait for me.'

'Of course I will wait for you. I know I have said it before but I *really* appreciate what you are doing for us at the Unit,' he said as she moved away.

Pip turned back and gave him the two-handed wave of victory. 'Jean-Luc, I've loved every minute of it,' she said with a smile.

As she was getting dressed Pip found herself thinking how happy she was. Jean-Luc was well on the way to full recovery, she had tied up several of the messy loose ends in her own life, the sponsored swim was going to be a great success and after that, there would always be other things to do – like helping the handicapped children learn to swim. Yes, that was the next goal to work towards.

Silently she thanked Jesus for her family and for her friends – in fact, for everything.